The Running Foxes is a story of
countrymen, the way they live, the
animals they love, the hounds they
breed. It is above all the story of a
vixen who teaches her cubs how to
hunt for themselves, and how to
escape from men and dogs. It is a
story which captures the reciprocal
devotion between men and dogs, and
the hard life of farmers in a barren
country where blizzards and floods
disrupt the lives of animals as well as
men.

'Joyce Stranger brings the smell of the
hedgerow and the sharp cry of the fox
in the night to her vividly written tale
of the wild creatures she loves.'—
Evening News

Also by Joyce Stranger

and published by Corgi Books

Joyce Stranger

The Running Foxes

Illustrated by
DAVID ROOK

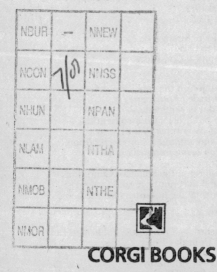
CORGI BOOKS

THE RUNNING FOXES

A CORGI BOOK 0 552 07600 7

Originally published in Great Britain
by Hammond, Hammond & Co. Ltd.

PRINTING HISTORY
Hammond, Hammond edition published 1965
Corgi edition published 1967
Corgi edition reissued 1972
Corgi edition reprinted 1974
Corgi edition reissued 1976
Corgi edition reprinted 1979
Corgi edition reissued 1983

This book is set in Georgian 11 12 pt.

Corgi Books are published by Transworld Publishers Ltd.,
Century House, 61–63 Uxbridge Road, Ealing,
London W5 5SA
Made and Printed in Great Britain by
Hunt Barnard Printing Ltd., Aylesbury, Bucks.

PREFACE

It is not possible to be English and remain unaware that in country places the Hunt plays an enormous part in village life.

It has a social function. In rich counties the Hunt is financed by an interested few of the county leaders, each paying a large subscription to keep the kennels running and the hounds trained and fed, and the Huntsman paid.

In poor counties the men own their own hounds, and a retired Huntsman or an amateur with time to spare will lead the pack. The Master of Hounds is a personage, his work a joy to watch.

Hunting has its opponents and its advocates. This book does not take sides. Whatever opinions are held, it is never possible to refrain from admiring the patient working of the pack, or the incredible cunning of the foxes, which, after centuries of hunting, are by far the most intelligent of British mammals.

There is no such place as Hortonmere, and the villagers and farmers only exist in imagination; but there are men who hunt for the joy of leading their hounds, not caring if the day end with a 'gone to earth' at dark, when the fox is left free, and all over Britain there are foxes running, employing wiles like those described in my book.

The fox is a killer, and often a thief, but even those farmers with most cause to hate him, speak with grudging admiration.

And so, the book begins, as does the Hunt, with a Find, and with a View. There are many checks as the hounds find the scent foiled, but the fox breaks cover and is Gone Away. At times he has also Gone to Earth, and many a time a Halloa gives the clue to his whereabouts.

At the end of the day the Hunt is baulked, and it was not the fox that found death in the morning.

CHAPTER ONE

RUFUS and Rusty became legends round Hortonmere, that autumn and winter. There are always foxhunting stories in a place where every man owns his own hound, but these were exceptions, all come from eye-witnesses. Many of them came from old Jasper Ayepenny, who always had an eye for what went on around him, but who was, this time, personally involved, for the foxes affected his life.

Jasper farmed in a small way at Bruton-under-the-Water, a village that owed its name to the falls that dropped over Horton Pike. Chickens and ducks fought the bare ground for a living. Five cows found meagre grazing on the grass at the edge of the peat bog. A one-eyed terrier and a ginger cat fought for the hearth-rug, and Jasper, at the beginning of that winter, was at odds with everyone.

Once he had hunted whenever the men went out, but now he was old. Worse, his terrier, Skim, a fierce fighter and a valiant dog, had been forcibly retired by the Hunt, who said that he was far too old to go out on the fells. The younger men had little time for Jasper, and were impatient with him, so that he became surly. He objected to the hounds crossing his land, and to the lads who climbed the drystone wall as they followed on foot, dislodging rocks that were often not replaced, so that the cattle wandered out on to the marsh which held death in its miry places.

Horton Hunt is not a colourful affair of mounted men, brave horses, and brilliant colour, but a Lakeland relative. The men in the Lakes hunt on foot, drab—clad in everyday gaberdines to keep off the rain that drenches down on eight days out of ten. There is no Master and no Pack, for the Lakeland farmers do not have money to spare. Each man breeds his own hound, and runs it and bets on it, and cashes in during the gloomy evenings when the day is over and men are gathered in the steamy firelit dark timbered room at the *Black Swan*.

The Huntsman wears fawn piped with red, and keeps a watch on his Pack, noting that Jim Turner's Bella runs well at the start of the day but soon tires; that Ned Thatcher's Flier is easily misled by rabbit scent or the quick flaunt of a pheasant tail over a pasture; and that Jamie Leigh's Swiftsure runs fast and fleet and is usually first at the kill.

Daylong, the men tramp tirelessly over bleak fells, climbing rocky slopes, dropping down sliding screes to streams where a cunning fox masks his scent in the water. At night, they relive each second of the day, from the breakaway across ploughed pasture to the quick double turn on the fern-clad hill, and the bold terriers digging the day's catch from a drain.

That year, the Hunt met its match. Not once did the hounds kill, and old Jasper listened, grinning slyly into his beer mug, as the frustrated farmers spoke of witchcraft and magic, and wondered if Bess Logan, down at Buttonskeele, had put the evil eye on them for the damage the hounds did when they trampled her rose beds.

Jasper's one-eyed terrier, Skim, and his ginger cat, Stalker, knew as much as anyone about the two foxes that laired up in the rocks on Burnetskill. The vixen had come running one March day, her left paw tattered where she had chewed herself free from a snare.

Skim sniffed the blood trail, and followed eagerly, He had once been one of the most daring Hunt terriers, but, like his master, he was old, and the younger men had no time for him. Jasper had taken the dog's forced retirement badly, and refused the Hunt permission to cross his land. They took scant notice, which increased his hatred for them.

The scent of blood roused Skim, and he chased through fern and heather, following the trail. He found the vixen lying in labour in a grassy dell, and barked at her angrily, so that she picked up the one born cub and ran, panting desperately. The cub was too newborn and not strong enough to stand such treatment and died. She left it reluctantly as she paused for the birth of the second.

She stood over the cub, snarling. The terrier approached, and the vixen sprang, her eyes glowing. She shrieked, and the peacock scream sent the old dog flying, his tail between his legs, startled out of his wits. The vixen picked up her cub and took it in her mouth to a deserted burrow, where she bore two more, of which one was dead.

The two remaining cubs grew fat on milk enough for six. But before their eyes were open they had a second adventure, for old Jasper, curious to discover just what had sent his terrier raving home, came poking about with a stick and found the earth.

He grinned to himself.

He saw that he could fool the hunt by masking the scent of the den with something stronger than fox. A few bucketfuls from the midden where he flung the cleanings from the pigsties would foil any hound. He walked home happily, keeping his knowledge to himself.

The vixen saw the poking stick and smelt the man behind it. She could not know that he did not mean to

drive her from her den, so she took precautions. She found an old hollow tree above the scree, with a little runnel of water falling from the hillside, slipping past the roots of the gnarled old-timer. The water would mask her scent as she crossed it, and the hollow was thick with fallen leaves and high off the ground.

Before the moon glowed high above the steely sheet of water that was Hortonmere, the vixen had carried the two cubs to safety, and when the owl rocketed down on the first unwary fieldmouse, she was safely curled round the pair of them, feeding them while she tore at an unwary leveret that had crossed her path.

The vixen was more cunning than most, and she taught her cubs well, so that they seemed, to those who learned their story, quite uncanny, and more than one who followed their trail wondered if they were, in fact, flesh and blood, and not ghost foxes sent by Bess Logan to bedevil the hounds.

CHAPTER TWO

THE tattered paw was partially healed, though the vixen always ran lame. It did not affect her speed. Jasper could identify her trail by the mark of the injured paw in boggy patches, and he soon saw from the following pad marks that she had two cubs.

Once, waiting in the night, he saw her coming down the scree, the cubs following. He watched her, knowing that she would not steal on her own doorstep. Her quarry would lie farther away. So long as her lair was near his home, he was safe from her depredations. He hoped she would make for Farthingdale, where the Tanners could afford to lose a hen or so. The Tanner boys were rare ones for knocking down Jasper's walls as they ran to keep up with the Pack.

The vixen had been hunted before. She came from Coniston way, and the Hunt had chased her on three occasions. She knew the need to show her cubs the land, so that they could take advantage of every piece of cover, of ditch, and drain, and badger holt.

She took them hunting, but she also took them by secret trails that led across stream and marsh. She taught them to track her by scent, and then, when they were almost on her, she cunningly leaped four feet in the air so that they lost the trail when she bounded, and quartered the ground desperately, trying to find her again.

Together they watched her fool the rabbits. The moon had almost set, and the last thin rays shone on a narrow grassy plateau high on Burnetskill, where the young bucks chased each other in dizzy spirals, so lost in their game that the fox was almost upon them before they saw her.

Almost, but not quite, for a paw thumped and the white scuts vanished, all except for one that faltered, too slow on the turn. The vixen did not pounce, as the cubs expected. Instead, she began to chase her tail, her reddish fur glistening where the dew clung to it. The buck came nearer.

Watching eyes saw only an innocent fox at her games. The cubs joined her, and the three of them chased and rolled and bit, ignoring the rabbits that crept out to watch, fascinated by such an unusual sight.

The cubs were puzzled. Their small noses wrinkled, filled with the entrancing rabbit smell. They could not understand their mother, but knew better than to disobey her. Her teeth were sharp and both cubs had been sorely nipped for unruly behaviour.

The bucks grew bold. Sure that they were unobserved, they advanced closer, anxious to see the unusual sight.

As the cubs rolled away from her, the vixen crouched, her white furry underparts almost pressed into the ground. One leap, a bite, and it was over, and the unwary buck was flung to the cubs while she caught a second, and fed full, not sharing her prize.

Jasper, rising as always when the sun came over the peak of Burnetskill, saw the three of them loping home, the two youngsters still skittish, the mother tired, her head hanging, her limp pronounced. They vanished in thick undergrowth, but not before he realised that the earth he had found had been abandoned. He wondered where she lay now, and determined to find out.

He called Skim, and the dog ran towards him, body ecstatic, tail waving, as he realised that the old man intended to take a rare walk.

They crossed the fox trail, and Skim's nose went down to it. He glanced at his master, and Jasper nodded.

'Find them, boy,' he said.

The terrier was overjoyed. Once more he was hunting, and the old skill remained so that he was soon level with the little trickle that led round the tree. Jasper looked at it, and then glanced thoughtfully upwards. Red hairs were caught in the bark. He saw the hole, and pondered, while the terrier watched him, unable to believe that there was not to be a kill.

That night, in the *Black Swan*, Jasper listened to talk of hunting. It was not yet time, but already the men were grooming the hounds, laying drag trails which they could follow. Jasper had met the Huntsman only that morning, with his sack that he pulled behind him, laying the scent strong and true.

'Matt Falcon's seen signs of a vixen and cubs at his farm,' said Josh Johnson, a giant of a man from Tedder's Leigh. His red beard spilled into his beer mug, and he laughed lustily. 'Killed three pullets. Matt took his gun,

14

but he didn't fire. She was well away. Lame,' he added. 'Short on one foreleg.'

'She'll be the beast that Brook Holler trapped,' said Jim Turner, a tiny fair-haired man with a thin ferrety face and blue eyes that watered whenever he went out of doors. He drank noisily, and his beagle, Bella, watched every movement, raising wise eyes under a broad benign brow, as hand went to mouth and back to table.

Jasper stretched in the chimney corner. The *Swan* was old when Prince Charlie was strampaging over the country, trying to rouse men to his banner. The long white-scrubbed table tipped to one side on uneven flags, and the ceiling above Jasper's head was a foot lower than it was above Ned's. The worn beams were black and shining with oil rubbed in to keep the worm at bay.

Mrs. Jones kept a two-gallon copper kettle boiling on the hob for those who needed tea. She was a homely woman with an applebun face and dark hair streaked grey that was tied in a loose knot at the back of her neck. People came from all over Cumberland to sample her food.

The Hunt came to tea at the end of a day's walking. Came to eat home-baked bread and farm butter, with rum butter and blackberry jelly, and great slices of ham served with lettuce and tomato and chutney made from a secret recipe.

They followed it with slices of apple pie, pastry melting in the mouth, and rich with cream from Dolly, the Jersey cow that browsed in the orchard. Lest their hunger were still unappeased, there were also scones the size of saucers and light and fluffy as summer cloud, and rich cherry cake, soaked in brandy, and, for those with more delicate palates, iced cakes and rock buns and Queen cakes deserving of a poem.

Jasper missed the Hunt teas, and Mrs. Jones took pity

on the old man, knowing that he roused impatience among her other customers. If he came to the *Swan* the day after a Hunt, there was always a bag of goodies to take home, and share with Skim, and with Stalker, the fierce one-eared Tom that kept him company when not hunting for delicate tabby brides.

He thought of these teas now as he drank his ale and sat silent in the chimney corner, toasting his rheumatism by the fire. The other men dismissed him as a silly old gaffer and ignored him when they talked of their plans, but to-night even he was included in the conversation for Tom Ladyburn had drawn a sweepstake ticket and was asking all and sundry for advice.

'Three hundred pounds now, whether I win or not,' he was saying. 'If the horse wins, I get two thousand. What'll I do?'

'Keep the money and don't be daft,' said Jim. 'If the horse don't win you'll not get a penny.'

'That's right,' Mrs. Jones agreed. She topped the beer mug and slapped it down in front of Jasper. 'What do you think, old man?'

Startled at being included, Jasper wiped his mouth with the back of his hand and turned to meet the grinning faces.

'Take the money,' he said. 'You with a wife and four lads. What are you thinking about? The horse won't win.'

The men broke into noisy advice. Flier barked, and Skim snarled at the tabby of the *Black Swan*, who was lying peaceably washing three ginger kittens. She spat, in an off-hand, disinterested manner, just to show that she had noticed him, and returned to her task. Skim nosed forwards, sniffed the kittens and to his astonishment, caught a faint whiff of Stalker. Bewildered, he crept back between his master's legs and put his whiskered face down on the shiny boot, and lay dreaming at the flames from the roaring coal fire.

'Keep the money,' Jasper repeated.

Skim, thinking he was being addressed, wagged his tail, and the tabby cat paused to stare with green eyes. She rolled herself round the kittens, but one of them escaped, and taking advantage of a moment's inattention, ran across the old terrier and clawed its way up to Jasper's knee, where it crouched, making a ten-gallon purr come from its pint-sized body.

'You're Stalker's kit,' the old man said, and rumbled with laughter as the little beast licked his hand.

'Take the money and don't be foolish,' Mrs. Jones said again.

'Take the risk, man,' Matt Falcon's rich voice boomed. 'Take the risk, and I'll lay you twenty to one the horse will win.'

'Forty to one against,' shouted Rob Hinney, a thickset, red-faced man who was cowman at Wellan's, the only farm with good soil beneath its grass, where sixty fat Jerseys grew sleek and made their master rich. Rob Hinney loved his herd, and knew each cow by name, rejoicing in each calf, and so quick to detect a cough or a trace of scour that there was rarely time for a beast to become sick where he was working. Catch an ill early, and it's no ill at all, was his maxim, and Ted Wellan paid him extra for the trouble he took.

'I'll give you fifty for the ticket,' the Huntsman said. Nobody ever remembered his name, and some thought he had forgotten it himself. He was a little dried-stick of a man with the bluest eyes this side of Windermere, a creased little face that only smiled at his small grand-daughter, and legs that had walked more miles in their time than any other legs in Britain.

The roars deafened the rafters and set the beagles

barking. Skim woke, sure he had been attacked, and snarled furiously, and the kitten climbed Jasper until it met the warm hollow between chin and shoulder and went to sleep again. The roars were cheerful and happy, for everyone knew that the Huntsman had not a penny beyond his pension and the bit the men could give him to help him out in his office.

'Fifty farthings,' Matt said grinning. 'Come on, man, keep the ticket and stand a round on the strength of it.'

'I've got five weeks to decide,' Tom said. 'I tell you what: Hunting starts in four weeks' time. If we kill the

first day, I'll keep the ticket. No, kill, and I'll turn it in, and hope the horse don't come in. Couldn't bear to settle for three hundred and then find I'd sent two thousand down a foxhole.'

'Lay you five to one we don't kill,' Jasper said, and grinned at the astonished faces turned to his.

'Done,' said Mrs. Jones, who felt sorry for the old man. He was bordering ninety, and though he was hale, he could no longer tramp the fells and follow the hounds, and she knew what his rejection by the younger men meant to him. She had asked them to invite him at least to the Hunt tea, but the men were thoughtless and the black fells did not breed kindness.

'We'll all end up the same way,' Matt Falcon had said.

'Have old Jasper, and no knowing where it will stop. And who's to pay for his tea? Not him, on his pension.'

The old terrier stretched himself as his master roused creaking bones from the creaking wicker chair. The men had forgotten him, and though he nodded as he went out into the chillness of dark, only the landlady acknowledged his exit.

'Fools,' he thought, cuddling his heavy coat around him and whistling his terrier. He had watched his foxes. He knew there had never been cubs like these on the fells round Hortonmere.

CHAPTER THREE

THE vixen was lying in a briar brake, her cubs near by. Although her eyes were half-closed, she was alert, her nose questioning the wind, her ears listening. A weasel, trotting down a dry ditch, caused her to raise her head, but she was not interested in him. Bones and feathers lay between her and the cubs, and on far-away Seven Pike a furious farmer stared, unbelieving, at the havoc wrought in his hen-run during the night.

Rusty, half sitting, half lying, his tongue hanging out as he remembered the night's killing, could see through the tangled thorny growth and out on to the fells. A turn of his head showed him an eagle, diving on its kill. Beyond the briar, in an ancient elm that was twisted with ivy, a little woodpecker hammered industriously. Knock, knock, knock, up to ten, a pause and start again. Far away his larger cousin sounded like a pneumatic drill thundering remorselessly on the branch of an ash tree.

Rufus was dreaming. His hind legs kicked convulsively, his pointed ears twitched, and a growl rumbled in his throat. It changed abruptly to a startled snarl as the vixen leaped to attention, knocking him with her forepaw by accident.

She knew the sounds, and looked quickly about her, trying to pierce the September haze that hovered wraith-like on the hill and drifted over the water. The echoing cries brought memory, and, also, fear. Not for herself but for her cubs, who were not yet fully grown, and needed training. As the faint baying of hounds came towards them from the Meet, she hissed at her young.

She had taught them well, and they watched her, waiting for a signal. When she loped through the bracken, keeping deep in cover, they followed, silent, Indian-file, avoiding the crack of stick and the rustle of grass, and keeping among stiff undergrowth so that waving fronds should not betray their passing.

Jasper knew that the men were hunting. He watched the old terrier stretch stiffly, hind legs, front legs, and then neck and head, and turn half-blind eyes towards him, begging to be allowed to follow the Hunt. The old man stroked the dog, and took him to the outhouse where he chained him firmly. Skim whimpered miserably and then lay down, resigned, unable to understand why, in this last year, he had been forced to lie at home while the other terriers and hounds ran over the fox trails.

Stalker, home after a three-day riot of his own, called a temporary truce and came into the shed and dropped companionably on to the straw, sprawling comfortably, lop-eared head on the old dog's back. Sensing the terrier's misery, the ginger Tom began to groom the rough coat, bringing a measure of comfort with his warm tongue. Jasper put down a plate of meat for them to share, and went out to watch, first checking his drystone wall. If the Tanner boys were following, he might need to put in a claim against the Hunt.

He brought the old Windsor chair out on to the porch and set it down in the sun, cursing his legs which no longer carried him as far as he wished. The five cows watched him curiously, finding much to wonder about. Jasper chuckled, remembering how they had once escaped and trampled his little garden. He had found Twitchett and Lou peering through his kitchen window, their wide rumps wriggling, tails switching as if they commented on his furniture and fixings and said to one another:

'Just fancy! So this is how people live.'

The vixen, stealing along a dry ditch that led to his wall, hesitated. Jasper, turning his head, glimpsed her sharp ears, and froze. The watching fox, after a minute's indecision, decided that the man was asleep, and because she was desperate and determined to foil the hounds, she called the cubs on with a soft hiss, and jumped the dry-stone wall, her young close behind her.

She was so quiet that the dog did not hear, and because the wind was wrong, did not scent her either. Jasper could not believe his eyes, as the three loped across his tiny garden, making for the midden. A moment later, he understood, and sat holding his laughter in, as he thought of the baffled hounds and the empty day's hunting.

The vixen ran to the midden and rolled. It was rich with the droppings of pig and cow and chicken, and ripe, and her cubs, taught to clean their glossy coats meticulously, could not believe their eyes. The vixen hissed at them.

Roll in that? Rusty whimpered, and his mother's teeth snapped within an inch of his ear. Reluctant, choking, and disgusted, the cub wallowed, and came out

22

hating the stink of his body, and the vile muck that clung. Rufus, meeker, less likely to disobey, did the job thoroughly, and Jasper was hard put to it not to laugh aloud as the three unseemly animals left as they had come.

The vixen did not risk the chance of the stuff's wearing away from her paws. She took the cubs to earth in a deep drain that tunnelled under the drystone wall, and led to a spot directly below the midden. No hound could possibly scent them there, and she knew that time would pass before the next Meet, time in which she could train the cubs better, and teach them her own wiles.

Jasper did not know that she had gone to earth almost beneath his garden, but he hugged the knowledge of her cunning to himself as the Pack found her trail and followed it down the fell. It led to the midden, and the puzzled hounds quartered the ground with worried expressions on their faces.

'Jasper Ayepenny,' Jim Turner asked, vexed, 'be you hiding that fox?'

'I know nought about the fox,' Jasper answered with a complete disregard for the truth. He suddenly found himself admiring her, and, with his own farm untouched, he even wished her well.

Skim, scenting the hounds, sent up an outcry, and this hardened his master's resolve.

'Mind my walls,' he growled, 'and get those damned hounds out of here, trampling and messing. There's no fox near.'

The Huntsman called them off, and the hounds milled into the lane, ears and tails drooping, puzzled bodies pushing against each other, as the familiar fox-smell drifted up from the dust. Bella went off alone, and Jim Turner went after her, threatening to beat her for disobedience.

'He's too soft with that bitch,' Ned Thatcher observed in his surly voice, and flicked a finger at his own animal. Flier came at once, a wary eye cocked for a kick, and Jamie Leigh glanced meaningly at the Huntsman, who avoided his eyes, not willing to criticise, even by a glance.

The foot followers sat along the stone walls, eating sandwiches, watching the hounds' efforts to find another scent. The cars parked high on the hill, their occupants eating in greater comfort, and jumping up and down with binoculars to see if another fox had been flushed from cover. Two men in racy tweeds, balanced on a white-barred gate, swapped stories of other foxes, of improbable hunts for tiger and elephant, and then began to talk fishing, their catches growing in size with every sentence.

The Huntsman called up the Pack, and set off across a ploughed field, clambered the ditch, pushed his way through a briar hedge, and out on to the bleak windy fell. The sunshine had gone, and clouds gathered in lowering heaps, piled dark and stormy, and reflected in the sullen waters of Hortonmere, now tipped with white flecks from a niggling wind that blew off the peaks.

The less ardent followers pulled up their collars and started for home. Only a handful were left when Swift-sure flushed a hare that had been lying doggo in a sheltered hollow, and as it loped off, long-leaping to-wards briar that would tangle the hounds and help it hide, the Pack bayed in pursuit.

The vixen, creeping out when the hounds were well away, sniffed the wind. She knew from the distant baying that there was quarry in sight, and she wanted the cubs to see the kill. Her own mother had shown her a hunted cub, torn apart in seconds, and the lesson had never been forgotten. In no other way could she impress upon her sons their need for wisdom.

She edged out of cover and on to the fell. Jasper, seeing her from the window, watched until she and her cubs were but distant shadows, climbing towards high heather tufts and thick briar patches. Each beast kept its distance. The smell of pig clung vilely, and several times the youngsters paused and rolled, trying to rub it off, but their mother harried them, anxious to keep out of sight and yet within seeing distance of the Pack.

She led them deviously, through a little wood where the trees were back-combed and flustered by perpetual wind, across six stones that bridged a turbulent stream that ran fast and yeasty with peat when rain cascaded in the hills. Rusty was tempted by the water and longed to sink his smelly fur in its clean depths, but the vixen guessed his purpose and, turning sheepdog, snapped quietly at his heels, driving him on.

She reached her goal, an inclined tree balanced on a rock, its branches still green and leafy, giving shelter from prying eyes. The last gale had uprooted it, and it was a favourite look-out post for many animals, giving a view down a rocky glen, and on to grassy meadow where fieldmouse and harvest mouse, shrew and mole all lived in close company, among rabbits and scattered hares. The owls often roosted here, watching for tell-tale movement, and Stalker, too, amused himself by observing the little creatures that crept below him, until he felt it time to pounce and play and tease, before he killed.

A squirrel had her drey here, and as the foxes dodged on to the trunk she shrank into a tiny crevice, forcing her small body into a crack that led to a larger hole. The vixen knew she was there, but did not bother. She advanced to the extreme end of the mossy trunk, and paused, looking back at the cubs. They followed her uneasily, not sure of her purpose.

The hare came into sight, fleeing over tumbled rocks

that were flung across the glen by swollen winter streams that tossed boulders as if they were made of sponge. The path was uneven, and devious, and the hare twisted and turned, leaping from side to side, struggling to defeat the Pack.

The hounds spilled into the glen, the leaders running strongly, Swiftsure only a head away from his quarry. Behind them the Huntsman came, watching each animal, marking its traits. There were many young hounds, out for the first time, and Jo Needler's Painter, an oddly-bred beast with ears too short, legs a shade too long, and a wretchedly-shaped muzzle, looked like challenging Swiftsure for the lead. A good stayer, the Huntsman thought. Far behind, little Madam, an undersized bitch with more humour than cunning, stopped to tease a frog that jumped, squeaking with terror, in front of her floppy paws Her master swore—one of Bella's pups, and she was no good either. He'd lost another bet to-day. He'd have to trade her for a decent hound.

High above them on the hillside, unseen and on the wrong side of the wind, the three foxes watched the hounds drive down the gully, Swiftsure leading the field. Painter, with an unlooked-for burst of speed, came ahead, and, using his wits, made a detour that served to corner the hare in the shelter of two vertical rocks. Terrified, the beast tried to leap them, but failed, and the Pack closed in.

The Huntsman was among them, beating them off, as they fought each other for the spoil. The cubs watched the Pack come to order, saw the men, eyes brilliant with excitement, descending into the valley, laughing, shouting, joking, now the day had had its climax. Bets were settled and new ones made and hounds compared, Jamie bragging about Swiftsure, challenged by Painter's owner. Jo Needler was a tiny man, dapper and miserable, who made a precarious living from a nursery garden that was overgrown with weeds and defied his efforts to keep it under control. Insignificant himself, he welcomed the hound's prowess, for a man gained stature when he owned a good beast. He made a mental vow to buy a large meal of liver for his animal on the way home.

It would soon be dark. Men and hounds turned wearily for the long walk back to the *Swan*. The vixen relaxed. Once more the fell was hers. She took the cubs to a shallow pool that led off the stream, and let them bathe. Some of the smell remained, clinging for days, reminding them of the Hunt and its end. The cubs now knew as well as the vixen that should the hounds find them unwary, death would come swiftly and brutally.

That night they hunted above Bess Logan's cottage, taking mice and small rabbits and an unwary partridge, leaving strictly alone the places where men lived. Daybreak found them deep inside a badger's earth, curled up close for company. The vixen showed them the way in and the way out and a further secret entrance that was reached by way of a bramble patch, so thick that no man could penetrate it and put in his dog to dig. It was well to know every bolthole on the fell. They would have need of them.

The cubs slept, rolled into a tight ball, one against the other, and the vixen licked her injured paw, which often pained her, and then slept and dreamed of fat geese and white ducks, until her dreams changed to nightmares, and she was once more chased by the hounds, flying for her life across scree and through heather. Her whimpering woke the cubs. They crept to her, and she licked each one in welcome, knowing that her time was short with them; for even if she avoided the Hunt, the day would come when she would leave them to fend alone, and seek herself a mate.

CHAPTER FOUR

THE story of the fox in the midden was too good to keep
to himself, and Jasper unwisely told Mrs. Jones when he
walked down to the *Swan* in the morning to collect his
share of the Hunt tea. The landlady, wrapping cakes
and pasties, listened and chuckled to herself. Her father
had often told her that foxes would roll in muck to mask
their own smell, but she had never believed him. Nor
had any of the men in the village, for Nat Jones had
had a wayward tongue, and often let a story run away
with him.

That evening, Jasper turned in for his pint, accompanied by Skim. Stalker followed discreetly behind, running through the gardens, and appearing, tail waving,
to press against his master and greet him, purring, delighted because for once he also was out for a walk.

'Go home, stupid,' Jasper said, irritated. 'There'll be rare laughter in the *Swan* if you come too.'

The cat waved his tail as if he understood, and giving Jasper a scornful glance, vanished down a side alley. When the old man reached the crowded kitchen that served instead of a bar room, the ginger cat was lying on the hearth-rug, a faintly-smug expression on his whiskered face, as one kit pulled his tail and the others investigated him thoroughly, finally settling on his back while the throbbing tabby curled against Stalker's white shirt, and licked his battered jaws.

The men sat on the settles round the table, the hounds lying at their feet. No man in Horton left his animal at home lest the women and children feed it titbits and spoil its wind. Those who could, took the hound to work. Those who could not, nagged their womenfolk, weighed their dogs, and when times saw hardship and scarcity, it was the family that went without the meat, while the hounds fed fat, and the wives grumbled at money wasted on dog-foods and betting.

Jasper walked into an atmosphere of cold hostility. Mrs. Jones had saved him his seat in the chimney corner, but even her smile and welcome, 'Come away and warm yerself,' did not make up for the eyes that followed him across the floor, or the foot that blocked Skim's path, so that the terrier snarled, and Wayward, a young puppy with more guts than sense, went for the old dog's throat.

Skim, brought up to battle fox and badger, turned his head. There was still power in his teeth, and they met, a fraction of an inch away from the youngster's jugular. Charlie Dee, a big bull of a man who bred bantams and fought them at a place that the police had been seeking for four years or more, gave a violent shout, and brought his hand down on the old dog's hindquarters.

Jasper moved with startling spryness, and clipped the terrier on the nose. When Skim let go, the pup retired, bleeding and whimpering, under the table.

Jasper lifted the terrier, who sat, growling, on his master's knee. The old man took his ale, and looked, from under shaggy white brows, at the men, waiting for someone to speak. He saw nothing but lowering faces, except for the Huntsman, who sat apart from the others, and would not meet Jasper's eyes.

'So they encourage foxes at Bruton-under-the-Water,' said Charlie Dee, mopping the blood from his whining pup. 'And they teach their dogs dangerous tricks there, too.'

'Your pup asked for it,' Mrs. Jones said. Not for nothing did she run her place single-handed, and deal with trouble before it arose. There was no nonsense at the *Swan*. Her sharp tongue kept the men in order, and before now her hand had dealt a hearty clip to any man trying a come-hither on her. Women were rare at the *Swan*. There was no money to spare to buy drinks for them.

Charlie looked away.

'So you let the fox roll in your midden and never lifted a finger to stop her,' Jo Needler said.

Jasper choked on his ale, and glared at Mrs. Jones.

'I'm sorry, Jasper,' she said unhappily. 'I didn't know they'd take it like this. I only thought...'

'What could I do?' Jasper asked.

'Set that dumb dog on her. Take a gun to her. Chase her off before she spoilt her scent and that of her whelps.' Jim Turner's face was red and a vein in his forehead bulged and thumped visibly.

'It'd do you no good if I shot her,' Jasper answered reasonably.

'You don't have to kill, you old fool,' said Charlie viciously.

'That's enough in my bar,' Mrs. Jones said sharply. 'Another word against Jasper and you go, the lot of you, closing time or not. I shouldn't have told you, but so help me, I never thought you were such a lot of children. One day's hunting spoiled and you behave like your own kids when the Sunday School Treat is cancelled. A fine lot of men you are!'

'You saw her roll, Jasper?' the Huntsman asked.

Jasper looked at him suspiciously, and he gave the old man one of his rare smiles.

'I'm not against you, old man,' he said. 'Give him another pint, Mrs. Jones.' He moved his place so that he sat opposite the fire, flames dancing on his weather-beaten cheeks. 'I'd heard the old tales, but never seen it done, and I'm interested. They say an old vixen over Basserdale had the same trick.'

Jasper nodded, and when the ale came he and the Huntsman were deep in fox-talk, recalling famous days in the past, and some of Skim's exploits. The men listened reluctantly and then, in spite of themselves, with fascination, as Jasper recalled the dogfox that climbed the Witches' Oak, leaped to an old elm, dropped through a coppice, crossed a stream, and holed up in a blocked ditch. Skim, put in to flush him, had come face to face with a polecat.

Jasper paused to drink, his nose wrinkling up reminiscently. Skim, hearing his name, flagged his tail gaily, licked his master's hand, and settled more comfortably, nose on rump, watching Stalker and the kittens.

'Not see many of those about now,' the old man said, aware that for once the younger men were listening. 'The gamekeepers saw to that. Worse killer than the fox, is a polecat. Go for goose and duck and turkey, and kill for fun. Kill every hen in the roost; and eat the brains of the last one. Eat anything. Eggs. Rats. Mice. Snakes. That one turned his back on Skim, and the terrier came out stinking and howling. Couldn't bear to be near himself for a week, poor beast.'

'Polecat? What kind of a beast is that now?' asked one of the younger men.

'Some call it a fitchew or a foumart,' the Huntsman said. 'Looks a bit like a longhaired otter. Not seen one since that day.' He laughed. 'Poor Skim! Hadn't an idea what to make of it.'

'Saw a skunk once,' said Jamie Leigh unexpectedly. 'In a zoo,' he added hastily, burying his nose in froth as everyone turned and stared at him. He was normally a very taciturn man. He swallowed. 'Don't want to get to windward of one,' he added. He glanced at Jasper. 'Reckon that fox is a sly one,' he said, and whistling to Swiftsure, went out into the night.

The Huntsman nodded to the men and followed him. Jasper stood up stiffly, after letting the terrier scramble to the ground. The watching eyes were less hostile, but for all that he went out without his usual salutation. Behind him voices broke the silence. He stumbled wearily up the hill.

He paused at the top to get his breath. Below him Hortonmere lay spangled by moonlight. Beyond it, out of sight, the vixen led her cubs along hidden trails that ended in a rabbit warren. She watched as both of them killed, and then found her own quarry. They were learning fast. She was well content as she showed them how to reach an old drain high on the hillside, following a wet gully that would hide their scent.

She showed them, too, how to watch as they ran, and use their noses, so that they were aware of the restless owl, of a prowling stoat, of a weasel dragging a rat, and

33

saw an inquisitive otter lift its head from the stream and sink swiftly, leaving a bubble trail glittering on the water.

They crossed Bess Logan's weedy garden. Her tiger-striped cat crouched, fur fluffed, tail thick, ears flat, and swore, eyes wicked, green, and vicious. The cubs paused, interested, but not alarmed. Rusty put forward an inquisitive nose, and the old warrior spat, raking the cub with a forepaw, so that blood spilled from his pointed muzzle. Brush down, he fled after his mother and brother.

CHAPTER FIVE

Sheerlings, where Rob Hinney tended the Jersey herd, was a rich farm. Ted Wellan's family had lived in the house for more than seven generations. An old house, with sloping ceilings, thick stone walls, and black oak beams, it had been built at the same time as the *Swan*. Rich forebears had filled it with dark antique furniture, which Christie's would have been proud to auction, and many men offered for the old black dresser, decorated by Mrs. Wellan with willow-pattern plates, and made splendid with the brilliant red and blue rosettes won by Ted's herd at the Dairy Shows.

There were ghosts at Sheerlings. The black barn, where an unlucky cowman had hanged himself over a century ago, was avoided by men and animals. Gloomy, open-ribbed, with the sky shining through its roof, it held an inexplicable atmosphere, as did the empty farm cottage where, every day, a woman's footsteps ran along the lane, turned in through the gate and tripped breathlessly in through the gaping front door, and up the stairs, and died away.

Oddest of all was the spirit that lurked in the End Room. Mrs. Wellan had had the End Room converted into a bathroom. It was handsome, with coloured bath and basin, red wallpaper on which tiny gold and silver pheasants flaunted in endless permutation, lavatory unit, and shining chromium shower. Yet on many days, the door was locked.

The first time this happened the Wellans counted heads. None was missing. The children watched round-eyed as Rob and their father forced the window and climbed inside to find the room empty and the door bolted. They removed the bolt and substituted a key. The key went, and a latch made from a hook and eye was put in its place. When even that was found fastened, all forms of locking the door were removed. The door jammed.

The Wellans gave up. The ghost seemed harmless in spite of its desire for privacy, and never troubled anyone who was there. The children insisted that an adult should hold the door open when they were inside. Unwary visitors were warned, but the mystery remained, and was all the more obscure because the unseen visitant came only at rare intervals, and without apparent rhyme or reason.

Ted kept pigs, sheep, and goats, also fat Rhode Island Reds that were not shut into battery cages but allowed to roam freely about the yard. Occasionally they invaded the big modernised kitchen, and the cock, in winter, often tried to find warmth by the big Aga, and was chased out, his mien indignant.

Jenny's pony, a delicate piebald named Miss Muffet, also frequented the yard, lifting the paddock latch when she smelled bread baking, and waiting with nostrils inflated, head daintily raised, well aware that no one could resist her charms.

Rusty, hunting alone, restless with youth, caught the scent of chicken on the wind, and sidled discreetly through the bracken, intent on his first solitary kill. He had left the vixen, with Rufus, above him on the fell. The vixen had a rabbit, and was growling over her victim, thinking it time her sons sought their own food. Rufus, unusually lucky, almost stumbled over a terrified leveret, feigning death. He refused to share it with his brother.

Rusty was starving. The wind brought him the farmyard smells, the scent of stoat, and the faint trace of a running deer, strayed from its usual haunts. He crouched low, his movements scarcely shaking the fern, finding his way by scent, rather than sight. He came to the edge of the farm as the moon lifted and rose, splendid, high in the sky, flooding the fells with light.

The farm was far from quiet. Ted Wellan had bought a new Jersey bull at the recent Beast Sale, and put it in a field above his cow-byres, where the land rose so steeply that the byre was built into the slope of the hill. He had not known the bull for more than a few days, and beyond making certain that the field was well hedged and the animal could not break out, he had concentrated on making friends, a task that seemed easy, as Jason the Golden was meek, overcome by the long journey in a rocking horse-box, and the bewildering unfamiliarity of his new surroundings.

This night he was more settled, and he heard a cow lowing in the byre below him, where Miranda had been placed because she had spent two hours in a deep ditch, almost under water. Dried and fed, and given an antishock injection, she had been put to keep warm. The herd instinct was strong in Miranda, and she called mournfully to her sisters.

Jason heard her, and investigated. It was plain from the exciting scent that she was in the byre, beneath him. He jumped the hedge, which was low here as the byre top was on the other side of it, and landed on the roof. This had not been built to taken a sudden weight upon it from above, and with a tremendous bellow that woke the whole family and brought Rob Hinney, half dressed, flying from his cottage, Jason fell through roof-felt and asbestos, and landed, supported by his powerful chest, across two rafters, his flailing hooves a foot above Miranda's terrified head.

As Rusty padded softly along the hedge bottom, Ted Wellan and Rob Hinney were pitching hay desperately on to the floor, urged on by the creaking and groaning of rafters that were about to break. The bull, silent now, watched them, his eyes intelligent as the piled hay mounted up beneath him. Mrs. Wellan, having brought the big Land-Rover and faced it to the byre so that its headlights flooded the scene, had raced to phone the Vet.

The Vet arrived, his car skidding to a stop, just as the bull gave a convulsive wriggle, freeing his front legs, and eased himself like a ballet dancer on to the hay. He stood for a moment, poised and gazing at them, and then dropped to his four hooves again and began quietly munching, apparently quite untroubled by his misadventure.

An examination showed nothing worse than a few scratches and a sore patch on the bull's chest, and the two men were drinking coffee, leaning on the Land-Rover, watching the bull and discussing the cow, when Rusty, hunger overcoming caution, broke cover and made for the chicken-house by way of the cow-field.

The smell of fox terrified the cattle. Lowing, they began to run towards the far corner of the field, as far away from the intruder as possible. Rusty hesitated, and in that second the Vet turned his head and whistled. Ted Wellan saw moonlight shining on chestnut fur, saw glinting eyes and mocking mouth, half open, tongue hanging, and the thick torpedo-shaped brush that waved defiantly as the fox stood. Then he ran for his gun.

As the cub came towards him, he fired, but missed. Rusty turned, flashed across the field, and went for cover among the cows. They tried to escape from him, but he followed, keeping a fat Jersey flank between himself and the farmer, driving the cattle, now terrified as he yelped and snarled, using them as a shield, until he reached the hedge bottom, and ran along it, creeping through to find his way, empty, furious, and shaken by the sound of the shot, back to his mother and brother.

That night, he fed on beetles, a small mouse, and three frogs, and he learned to leave Wellan's Sheerlings in peace.

CHAPTER SIX

JASPER, as the nights grew shorter, so that he, and the
rest of the men, went ever earlier to the *Black Swan*,
where they found warmth and company as well as good
beer, discovered another ally. Tom Ladyburn, good as
his word, had taken the verdict of the first day's hunting,
and chosen the smaller amount of money, rather than
risk losing all by keeping the horse that he had drawn.

When the horse came in a lagging sixth, Tom thought
of his small nest-egg and thanked his stars that the
vixen was cunning. But for her, he would not have that
money safely in the bank, against bad days and illness,
and lack of work.

He stood Jasper a beer.

'You and your foxes!' he said, grinning, and rubbing a nervous hand through his grey-speckled thatch. 'If it weren't for them foxes I'd a kept the durned thing. Reckon the vixen's brought me luck.'

'Reckon she has,' Jasper answered, and drank gratefully. His small pension did not run to more than a frugal half-pint in one night.

Rob Hinney, stamping mud from his boots, and shaking rain from his coat, flung through the door, shouting that he had a thirst on him fit for an Emperor.

'Sit down, man, do,' said Mrs. Jones, as Rob paced the kitchen, looking at the hunting-prints that decorated the walls.

Rob yawned.

'Been up half the night,' he said irritably. 'Feel as restless and as itchy as a moulting adder. That bull!'

He plunged into the story, drawing laughter as he gave a gusty and graphic description of the Wellans' champion bull dangling from the rafters. He went on to describe the fox's antics with the Jersey herd.

'Too wily by half,' said Josh Johnson. 'Niver known a fox so cunning. Mark my words, they're not the common run of foxes.'

'Common enough,' the Huntsman said, coming out of a deep abstraction on hearing the last words. 'I remember when I was a boy . . .'

His voice trailed away as he relived the past, suddenly remembering the feel of deep frost on the ground, the way the ice bit into numb fingers as they carried buckets of warm water to the sheep and the water froze on the handles before they reached the field.

There had been foxes then. Several of them, coming to find food on the farms because rabbits were dead in frozen burrows and there was little enough for any beast to eat. Running in broad daylight among the lambing flocks, quick to pick out the weaklings, bold as tame cats, and twenty times more destructive.

They had waited with the guns. And day after day, the foxes hid among the sheep, driving them like dogs, keeping always in the thick of the flock, so that nobody dared fire among the terrified, close-packed animals.

'Dodged and twisted and never gave a gun a chance,' he said, trying to describe the scene and give it the flavour of boyhood, of grey skies, heavy with snow, and the first whirling flakes blotting out the fells. The crisp rattle of frosted grass, the brittle stalks of heather, fairy-like in the sun, silvered with rainbow crystals, and then dully leaden as the sky clouded and the snow drove towards them. The hidden foxes, visible only by a gleam of red fur or a flash of bushy brush as they worked their will on the silly sheep.

Jasper remembered that winter. He had been courting, ready to marry late in life, but she'd have none of him. His sister kept house for him, and would brook no other woman. He wondered now as he wondered then if her sharp tongue had scared the girl away. A good girl. What was her name? Jennifer? The name had gone, but he could still visualise her quiet smile, and her soft voice, so gentle after his sister Mildred's harsh nagging tones. He sighed, watching the flames. Mildred had been dead this many a year, and most of his friends too. It was hard to live in a world and know that everyone else in it was too young to remember events that were still clear as the Horton Pool.

'Saw a fox swim the Mere one day,' Josh Johnson said. 'Came in at the far end where the fall begins, and swam clean across. Thought it was a dog until it landed.'

Eyes turned to the door as it opened and rain and wind swept in along with a newcomer. He nodded, with a wry grin, a little bent fellow, his wrinkled face dirty, his brown eyes dancing with unholy glee as the assembled men stared at ragged clothes and torn shirt, held together at the throat with a sky-blue scarf. His old coat was tattered, but thick, and something moved in the pocket.

'Ned Foley,' the Huntsman said. 'Where have you been these last months?'

'Down to Kendal, seeking a fortune,' Ned said slyly. 'I'm glad you offered me a drink, Huntsman, I'm skint.'

The Huntsman nodded to Mrs. Jones, who set her mouth.

'Time you found a proper job, Ned Foley, and stopped tramping the roads,' she said.

'I don't like being tied, woman. And I mind my own business,' Ned said pointedly. He put his hand in his pocket. 'Nobody can guess what I've got here.'

'Like to bet?' asked Josh Johnson, his bright eyes excited.

'Skint,' Ned said briefly.

'Bet a tanner I guess before you, Josh Johnson,' Matt Falcon said in his deep voice.

'It's a rabbit,' said the Huntsman.

Skim, who had been lying at his master's feet, one bored eye on the room and the other half shut, sat up and sniffed. His brown eyes snapped. He moved his muzzle, pointing, trying to find the source of the delectable smell that had suddenly filled the room. The other dogs and the hounds began moving uneasily, and Bella whimpered softly.

'Fox,' said Jasper.

'More like Ned hisself, the beast's smelling,' Josh answered, and chortled at his own wit.

Skim stretched carefully, easing his hind legs, which were stiff and rheumaticky. He trotted across the room, and stood with his forepaws on Ned's knee, his busy nose working. A triumphant second later he put his muzzle into the wriggling pocket and emerged even more swiftly, with a yelp and a bleeding nose. Crestfallen, he crept back to his master to be comforted.

Ned took a small beast from his pocket.

'It's a ferret,' said Mrs. Jones.

'Otter cub,' the Huntsman corrected. He put out a tentative finger, and warily touched the rough coat. 'Hullo. Damaged paw?'

'Another one from Brook Holler's trap,' Ned answered. 'He had a whelping fox a while back. Half chewed her foot away before I freed her. Don't hold with traps. Like putting a man inside four walls. It ain't natural.'

Mrs. Jones brought warm milk and a fish head, and the men watched the otter eat and drink. Sated, it turned and tried to climb back into Ned's warm pocket. He let it find sanctuary.

'So you freed the vixen,' Rob Hinney said.

'Thinking of the season's hunting,' Ned answered from the depths of his tankard.

'But not of our chickens,' growled old Tanner.

'Build your fences strong and your chicken-houses good, and the foxes won't get 'em,' Ned said provocatively. 'No use blaming the beast when your own bad workmanship and laziness is to blame.'

'Be damned to you, Ned Foley,' old Tanner shouted. 'Never a day's work in you and you dare to give advice to the rest of us!'

'The onlooker sees all,' Ned answered. His tiny, pouting, gap-toothed mouth spread in a disarming grin. 'I'll be off to me mansion, and thank you for your hospitality.'

He went out into the night, slamming the door behind him, and the mocking, mock-genteel phrase that had been deliberately chosen to annoy, hung on the air.

44

'Whisht, now, Mr. Tanner, I'll thank you not to burst a blood vessel in my bar,' said Mrs. Jones, wiping a clean cloth across the pockmarked table. 'You know as well as I where Ned Foley lives when he's at home. It's nothing to be jealous about.'

Ned lived in a hut on the fells above Hortonmere. Three walls were made of odd pieces of corrugated iron, picked up on a dark night from a far-away scrap-yard and brought home by the hang-headed pony and ramshackle cart that he occasionally used to collect rags and bones and scrap. The fourth side was of sacking, hung on old fence-poles, and his only fireplace was a coke brazier, 'found' long ago beside a steamroller on a road-mending site. Dry heather, peat, and wood brought in from the Farthing Forest kept Ned warm when he chose to live at home. The farmers on the fells would have liked him evicted, for they suspected that their chickens and ducks suffered as much, if not more, from his hands than from the foxes, but the fells were no-man's land, and nobody had power to move him on.

It was Ned, cooking bacon over his brazier on a frosty autumn morning, who saw Rusty's latest achievement. When he told it, nobody believed him. Not even though Jasper witnessed it, too.

The little man was whistling softly under his breath when he heard the beating of wings. Looking up, he saw the duck struggling against wind, making for water. Their sad voices called down to him as they flew. He watched the strong bodies and extended necks, feeling an odd excitement, as flight after flight flew in V-formation, and settled on the pool.

There was another watcher on Hortonmere. The vixen kept close to home, as infection had started in her injured foot. The swelling and pain kept her from straying far, and often the cubs hunted for her and brought her food, and watched her with worried faces, unable to understand why she did not join them.

Rufus, more loving and less bold than his brother, kept by her side, leaving her only long enough to find food, which he always shared. Rusty, growing faster and larger, was developing into a big dogfox, with a large frame and an appetite to match. He avoided farms since the night that Wellan fired at him, and found his food among the heather where partridge and rabbit kept him fed but not fat.

He had also learned that many creatures were almost as cunning as he. Not every rabbit fell prey. Some could twist and turn and leap and bolt, keeping cool heads that sent them running into burrows with many turns, burrows too small for a fox to follow without lengthy digging that usually revealed only an empty run.

Birds took to the air when he tried to catch them. Ducks suddenly submerged, or flew away. He stared hungrily across the mere, at the hordes of upturned tails wriggling enticingly. His mouth watered.

Hortonmere was a bleak stretch of mirrored grey, un-protected by trees. At the far end, water tumbled into it down a rocky face, filling the air with smoky foam. The banks were bare of reed and of weed, and the rocky shore was completely devoid of cover.

Only in one place was there any vestige of growth, and this was a narrow gully, where bramble grew thick-ly, and where, on the shore, a twisted stretch of dry grass met a patch of water-lily, now a tangled mat of drying stems and brown, rotting leaves.

Ned grinned as he saw the fox crawl across the stones, a brilliant patch of reddish brown moving over grey scree. The lithe body covered the ground rapidly, and the old man realised that the beast was making for the gully. A heron, flying from a distant nest in search of food, hovered to look at the unlikely sight, but, finding it of no possible interest, flew on, head humped and heavy wings slowly flapping.

Rusty covered the last hundred yards in a running flash, and was gone, hidden in the twisted tangle. Ned hastily made his bacon into a thick sandwich with bread and margarine, and, eating as he walked, stalked swiftly, noting the wind, until he had the head of the gully in sight where it met the shore.

The fox emerged, ran down the beach, and entered the water without a splash. Ned plunged down the gully in time to see Rusty swimming strongly against the current from the falls, a thick tangle of matted weeds covering the jaunty head. A moment later he was joined by Jasper, who had been gathering dry heather for kindling higher up the hill, and had seen the fox and come down to look.

The ducks did not see the weed that bore down upon them so swiftly. There was nothing to show danger, for the fox was swimming against the wind. A tiny ripple was left in his wake. Jasper held his hand over Skim's jaws as the terrier whimpered, scenting the rank, familiar smell.

It was over in a second. The fox took his prey as the drake dived, tail up, head down. There was a swift flurry, a strong beating of wings as the rest took fright and flew off, feet skimming on the water. Rusty discarded his improbable hat, and with the struggling bird in his jaws, swam shorewards.

The last the men saw of him was a waving brush as he ran slowly up the hill, jaws weighted by the fat drake that now hung lifeless, feathers trailing through the twisting heather stalks.

Jasper looked at Ned and the tramp looked back, grinning.

'He deserved that,' he said, and Jasper nodded.

'Wonder if Huntsman knows that trick,' he answered, shifting the heather bundle into his other hand.

'If he don't, he'll not believe you,' Ned answered, as he climbed back to finish his breakfast.

Jasper whistled to Skim, and walked wearily homewards, seeing Rusty once more, as the dogfox, having eaten his fill, took the rest of the duck home to the vixen. She, hot and restless, her paw burning, was able to make only a token meal, and while the cubs slept she lay staring out at the fells, sad-eyed, unable to understand what was happening to her.

CHAPTER SEVEN

Madam, the little bitch belonging to Jo Appleyard, had been shut in the toolshed. She was bored. She explored the floor, rubbing her nose in the dust until she sneezed, meditated briefly over a sack of potatoes before deciding they were inedible, and then lay, nose on paws, eyes forlorn, watching the door. When Roger Appleyard came in to find potatoes for dinner, and forgot to close the door tight, she was off in a second, across the tiny garden, over the drystone wall, and out on to the fells.

The day was hers. She needed a companion, and set off to find one. She found Bella, confined and miserable, whining in a barn. Madam began to dig under the rickety walls, and the older bitch, suddenly realising that freedom lay within reach of her paws, nosed frantically at the brittle wood, rotten with rain.

Black noses met and rubbed. Earth and splinters flew,

and soon Bella, too, was outside, dancing off to unwonted freedom.

They had the sense to run far from home before indulging in play. High on the fells, where the heather hid the rabbit runs, they ran in giddy circles, bounding through the tussocks, heedless with excitement. Bella started a rabbit, chased it, and then sat down, not hungry and not caring, her mocking tongue lolling out of her open mouth.

Madam found a fox trail, and drifted along it warily, nose to ground, stern waving. The wind blew into her face, her brown eyes gleamed, long ears flopped forwards as her low body swung through the heather. Rusty, asleep after a night spent hunting, heard the swift pad pad of her paws and raised his head, prick-eared, anxious, nose working agitatedly because in spite of the noise there was no alien scent to warn him of the intruder's nature.

A moment later he saw Madam, and she glimpsed his brush and gave excited tongue so that Bella left her own game and ran headlong, paws thumping on stony path. Rusty jumped to his feet. The vixen was lying in a tiny cave, Rufus with her. He knew instinctively that if the hounds scented her she would not have a chance, injured as she was. His brush lifted, he turned and loped swiftly in the opposite direction, showing himself fully.

The two hounds checked, looked thoughtfully at the running fox, and began to follow. Behind them, the vixen slept safely. Rusty determined that he would lead them on a long trail.

He chose to run upwards while he was fresh from sleep, picking his way over loose pebbles that rolled on a long scree. The hounds, both unfamiliar with the terrain, trod gingerly as they slipped on pebbles that rolled unnervingly down the hillside. Once a tiny avalanche of dust and soil swirled from under Madam's feet and dropped over a tiny cliff, taking with it a small, sparsely-rooted bush that twisted and tumbled, root over top, until it plunged on to the stony shore of Horton-mere, scaring the ducks, and a fishing heron that flew off above the lake, in order to make sure that no other missile should hurtle from the skies.

Rusty found a narrow rocky gully, the floor slimy with weed that grew in a trickle of water. Looking back, he saw Bella and Madam pushing their way through brambles that bordered the crack, trying to head him off. He scrambled hastily towards the head of the hill, where the going was smoother, and came up on the peak, silhouetted briefly against the light, before he turned and headed, heels flying, down the broken path that led back to the fell.

The hounds had forgotten everything except their quarry. Rusty led them farther from home, taking them into the next valley, through Wellan's rich farm, where the cattle grazed the only pocket of fertile soil within miles, through the pigs and piglets, scattering, grunting, and screeching with terror, through the field where Jason grazed happily, a group of heifers at his disposal, and, startlingly, before he had realized it, into the haunted barn.

Dust was thick, and he scattered it, his paws leaving marks that remained plain for days, and caused Rob Hinney to scratch his head and wonder if foxes were immune to atmosphere. Not even the cats came near the old barn. Had Rob been watching, he would have seen the fox baulk, circle uneasily, and, yickering with panic caused by something unseen, make hurriedly for a gap in the wall on the far side of the barn. Neither Bella nor Madam had followed him. They backed away, snarling, and waited, until Rusty appeared. He clambered over a wire-mesh fence, and dropped into a deep ditch which hid him.

Nobody saw Bella or Madam. Had they done so, their freedom would have ended. As it was the pair of them raced to head the fox from the end of the ditch, and were startled to see him double back and emerge again where they had left him, flying once more among the pigs, so that, up at the farm, heads looked from the window, speculating.

Rusty found a thick brake of briar behind the midden. He crouched there, panting, his scent masked by the powerful smell of pig and sow and horse, and the two hounds circled baffled, as they sought to find his scent.

When he broke away again they were far behind, but raced to cut him off. He found the river, almost dry, and crossed it twice, hiding once in a fallen tree that the children used as a bridge. Bella chased him out of that, as she crashed uncleverly among the branches, so that he dropped to the ground and flashed along a turfy path, its softness kind to hot pads lacerated by stones.

He was tiring, and so were the hounds. He looked back over his shoulder as they panted towards him, determined to catch him before the day was over. The sun, at its noonday height, was warm for the time of the year, and he wanted a drink. He stopped, and dropped his muzzle to a tiny pool of water caught in a deep rut, but allowed only a few drops to touch his tongue. Far away down the valley a string of ponies, ridden by children, trotted away from the Riding School, and the instructor, looking up, saw the fox turn and head towards the crags again.

There was a deep burrow where badgers had once lived, now empty except for the occasional fox. It led downwards, a mass of tunnels and ramifications, and ended in an old, deserted, and broken drain. The vixen had shown it to her cubs one day in September, knowing that it might well give safety on some distant date.

The fox leaped carefully over a boggy patch, dived into a culvert and vanished among the bracken, only the bending fronds showing where he passed. The two truants followed, noses down, careless of everything except their quarry. They were less wary than he when crossing the bog, and twice Madam floundered miserably in thick mire that clung to her legs. Bella, seeing her companion's plight, used her teeth on the smaller animal's scruff and dragged her clear. They went on, not knowing how close Madam had been to death. Behind them the bog closed again over its secret depths.

An old oak tree lay across the entrance to the burrow, its rotting stump a haven for ants, who had tunnelled in the bright brown wood. Rusty's paws, scrabbling on the surface, broke away a large chunk, exposing the straight drills, the scurrying creatures as they ducked into cover to avoid the light, and a number of juicy larvae, now in full sight. His tongue licked over them rapidly, but he heard the heavy pads behind him, ducked beneath the tree, and into the welcome darkness.

The tunnel opening was wide, and both Bella and Madam followed without hesitation, although neither of them cared for the dark or the dank smell of damp earth that came chokingly towards them. There were fox traces and rabbit traces, but they clung to the trail doggedly, following Rusty deeper and deeper under the ground.

Soon they were beneath the shoulder of the hill. The fox circled several times so that his trail was confused, and then struck out for the old drain. The hounds followed.

Inside the drain was wet, and he splashed through it and out on to the hill. There was a fast-flowing stream tumbling the boulders, where the clear water raced over rounded rocks and thrust between craggy banks. The fox splashed along for a distance of more than a hundred yards before once more regaining the bank and taking a short cut home.

Twice he looked behind him, but there was no sign of pursuit.

Nor could there be, for as he left the drain, forcing his way upwards before turning towards the stream, he dislodged wet soil and boulders, which grew into a landslip and blocked the end of the tunnel. The two truants found themselves facing a thick wall of earth, and although they tried to dig, there was insufficient room, and they were forced to give up.

Disconsolate, out of breath, exhausted by the long run, they lay, noses on paws, and slept. Waking, they retraced their steps, only to find that at the point at which the fox had circled, they could not pick up the trail. Madam took a wrong turning, and Bella followed. Soon they were hopelessly lost inside the hill.

Ned Foley saw the fox lope wearily past his hut, but did not give it a second thought. Later, he met Jo Appleyard looking for Madam, and remembered the weary beast. Casually, he suggested that Madam had been chasing on her own. Jo gave up the search temporarily and met Jim Turner, who was looking for Bella.

They turned into the *Swan*, anxious about their hounds. Jasper fondled Skim thoughtfully, and recalled that two hounds had passed him in the distance as he hunted for firewood. He had thought that they were strangers and not given the matter a second thought.

The Huntsman sat and listened. No man liked to lose a dog, and he pondered for a moment before suggesting that they took Swiftsure and Flier and Painter, all quick to follow a scent, and tried to trail the hounds.

The *Swan* emptied as the men went home for torches, and Jamie Leigh, Ned Thatcher, and Jo Needler brought their hounds, leashed, to Jim Turner's cottage, where the hole in the side of the old barn told its own story. The cottage was part of the old Home Farm, now long sold, and the barn stood on land that was soon to be used for a Council Estate, but as it backed on to the cottage garden and stood empty it had been agreed that Jim could use it for storage until it was pulled down.

Flier picked up the trail, and Painter and Swiftsure followed, pulling eagerly, out over the fells, up the scree, which defeated the men, who had to loose the hounds and let them follow alone. The Huntsman, afraid they might lose them in the dark, had come too, for all the Pack obeyed his call readily, and the rising moon shone on men and beasts strung out over the fells, as the search progressed.

Not until midnight did they reach the hill. Here Painter barked, having caught a sound from deep inside, and faint and far below the men heard an answering bark. They found the entrance to the earth beneath the old tree.

Ned Foley joined them and looked down at the hole.

'There's only one terrier alive can work through that,' he said. 'You want old Jasper's Skim.'

'He's too old,' the Huntsman said. 'It wouldn't be fair. There are other terriers.'

'None near so good,' Ned answered, glancing sideways under thin wiry eyebrows that stood out from his forehead almost at right angles.

'Jasper won't let 'un go,' Jo Appleyard said with conviction. Madam was the first hound he had owned, and he was fond of her, even though her frivolous ways often displeased him. The Huntsman had promised that when she was older she would be as good as the best of them.

He watched Swiftsure enviously. It seemed very likely that he would be without a beast of any kind. The faint yelps were deep underground, and Jasper was no friend to any of them. They had been too careless of the old man's feelings.

As they stood round the entrance to the earth, Rusty crossed within a hundred yards of them, walking like a cat, so that not even Painter sensed him, as the fox knew well how to watch the wind. The men huddled into overcoats. It was cold, a hint of frost in the air.

'You need Skim,' Ned Foley repeated, and Jim Turner longed to hit him.

'Come on, Ned. Let's see what we can do,' the Huntsman said. 'If Jasper won't let the terrier try, I'll be surprised. He's a kinder man than many of you.'

He went off, stiff knee'd, a weary little man at the end of a long and difficult day. Ned followed him, a Puckish shadow, oddly decorative in his tattered and improbable clothes. The men smoked and waited, listening to Bella's distant barks.

High above them, deep in cover, Rusty flushed a partridge, and ate it at once. He found a second, half an hour later, and made a cautious detour, reaching the vixen just as Ned and the Huntsman began to talk to Jasper.

The vixen looked at the partridge with lack-lustre eyes. She wanted water. She crawled out on to the hillside, and found a puddle. She drank eagerly, and then her strength failed her, and she lay, a bright and obvious target, sprawled on grey rocks in the moonlight. Rusty and Rufus pushed at her with their muzzles, whimpered at her anxiously, and then retreated to the dark safety of the cave, and watched miserably, not knowing what would happen next.

CHAPTER EIGHT

Moonlight picked out the dark hummocks of the smaller peaks as Ned and the Huntsman plodded over the rough ground, picking their way among rocks and tussocks. Twice they detoured along a field to find a gate, and once climbed wearily over a stile let into the drystone wall, made from uneven rocks piled one on each other with cunning balance, kept in place by their own weight, without a drop of mortar. They were on Tanner's land, and his man had finished the top with edge slates that gleamed dull blue in the soft light.

Behind them the huddled men waited, a clump of bushes giving them shelter. There was an occasional faint red glow as a man drew on his pipe, and the white coats, patched with lemon and tan, of the three hounds showed up with startling clearness as they nosed the ground restlessly, picking up the trails of mice, of weasels, of a mole that found poor going in the stony soil, and the overhanging rank smell of fox mixed with that of the trapped hounds.

Ned and the Huntsman walked with long unhurried steps, and without words. The Huntsman was thinking wistfully of the days, now long past, when he had been in charge of one of the real Lakeland packs. Fifteen couples hunted under him from September to March, covering the ground three times a week, in rain, frost, or even light snow.

There had been some wonderful hounds. Trier and Bennet. Joss Lincoln had walked Mocker every summer. Joss was a good walker and hounds in his charge were not overfed, and were well exercised. They accompanied him round the farm, and in the evenings he took them on to the fells where they often found their own trails and hunted alone, gaining strength and cunning.

He remembered Shiner. Shiner had been a great hound, a fine stayer and a good jumper. An ideal animal in every way, his body light and not running to heavy bone, his hindquarters well developed with long pasterns that sloped backwards, and hare feet.

He smiled, remembering the arguments in the *Swan* at night. The fell hound is like no other, for fell hunting is something on its own. A light hound can run well and jump high, and if his body is neat and his legs short, he can tuck them in and race over obstacles in high clean leaps, as if he were travelling over level ground, and with as little effort.

A heavy rangy hound, with one or two exceptions, found himself tiring on the rock hills. When he jumped, he landed badly, jarring his body and taking the shock, absorbing it in thickset shoulders. If he added cat feet and straight pasterns to solid bone and long legs he was useless on the climbing runs, and hopeless on a full day's hunt, for he wearied soon, and slowed down, his legs aching.

Painter was a little heavy, his legs perhaps overlong, but he had hare feet, like those of the coyote, the wolf, and the fox, so that he stood well, and had a long surface which took his weight evenly. He had, too, the shallow pads that showed no sign of wear even after a hard run, and well-developed dew claws that would help him cling when he had to scramble on the screes. The Huntsman hoped to see Painter develop into one of the memorable hounds, the next winter.

As he walked, he noted the trails that would take a fox to safety. The long line of a hill, the lie of a drain, the ditch close beneath a stone wall, cover afforded by bush and bramble. They rounded a heather-covered ledge. Looking down he saw that it afforded a good view over the valley. A fox might lie there unobserved, watch the hounds start off, and be away.

Below the bink, he saw a borran, a deep-rock earth. He did not know that the two young foxes lay inside, listening to the heavy clump of the two pairs of boots. He did not turn his head. If he had, he would have seen the vixen, now in the shadow cast by the rock above her, exhausted and listless, her life ebbing away. Ned saw her, and made a mental note. He would be back later to investigate.

Ned's thoughts were not on hunting. He had noted the silver back of a jumping salmon in the little river, and marked it down. An hour with a net should see it his. He knew the pool where it lay. He would find it sheltering beneath the rocky overhang above the weir, hidden from the noonday sun by a spreading stunted willow.

The moonlit night and the heavy boots of the man

walking beside him took him back to his own childhood when he and his brother were driven, weary and shivering, from their beds by their father. The old man had a hard tongue and a harder hand which he reinforced, when annoyed, by the buckled end of his belt. He had a peppery, unreasonable temper and was often annoyed.

Ned remembered the quiet trail through the silent woods, startled now and again by the hoot of an owl, and the feel of bramble and thorn catching at bare legs and naked feet. Silence had been imperative. There were gamekeepers in the woods, with orders to shoot intruders.

Safe in his father's pocket was a length of penny elastic, bought from the village shop that sold nuts and bolts and hayrakes, food and clothes, sweets and stamps, wool and turpentine, muddled up, higgledy-piggledy, so that the old man with white hair and long white drooping moustaches took hours to find what he sought, and bent under the counter muttering to himself angrily.

A visit to the blacksmith by the boys rewarded each of them with the offcuts from the horseshoes, tidy nuggets of iron, that had many uses.

Old Tom Foley had never worked in his life, but his family fed better than many of those who laboured from daybreak till midnight, as he had skills unknown to the virtuous. Now, as they crept from shadow to shadow, avoiding dry sticks and rustling grasses, Tom whistled, a soft, gentle sound that caused a hen pheasant to lift a startled face. A piece of iron fitted into the elastic found an instant target and the hen dropped like a stone. Ned and his brother crawled swiftly into the tangle of thorn and nettle to seek the hidden bird, preferring scratch and sting to the bruising efficiency of their father's belt, aided by a well-aimed kick, should fear of natural hazards deter them from the search.

The memory had been so vivid that Ned was startled to find himself at old Jasper's gate. The cottage drowsed in moonlight. Stalker lay along the wall, finishing off a mouse that had not moved swiftly enough from beneath his questing paws. Inside the cottage Skim lifted his head and barked. The Huntsman knocked.

It took time to rouse Jasper from sleep. He stood at the door presently, a startling figure in red-flannel pyjamas provided by a niece in London who wrote to her uncle every Christmas and kept him supplied with warm underwear and sleeping apparel. His white hair stood on end, and with his beaky nose, gave him the appearance of a crested crane.

The Huntsman did not waste words.

'Why should I risk Skim?' Jasper asked.

'I risked my terrier for yours, the year that the Queen was crowned,' the Huntsman said. 'I have no terrier now, or I'd put him in. Skim can do it.'

'He's losing his nerve,' Jasper said. He rubbed his unshaven face with an irritable finger. 'Came up against the vixen and turned tail and ran.'

'Shows he's still wise,' Ned interrupted. 'Vixen's injured and she was carrying cubs. She'd scare any creature off.'

Skim came to the door and thrust his cold nose into Jasper's hand.

'Fifteen years,' Jasper said. He stroked the rough head lovingly. He was proud of his terrier, a leggy, narrow-chested, brown-coated dog with a good muzzle and the remains of good teeth. Skim had fought underground many times, and come out happily.

'There isn't even a fox down there.' The Huntsman looked up over the fells. The moon was setting, its round rim showing coyly between two rounded hills. Frost was riming the grass and nipping the last roses.

Ned walked into the cottage impatiently.

'You'll catch your death,' he said to Jasper, whistling with his little pouting mouth open so that the air hissed between his teeth. 'Come on, man. We can take the dog. Get back to your bed.'

'He goes with no one but me.'

Jasper began to dress, his hands maddeningly slow, so that the Huntsman itched to help, but instead he busied himself making tea, and they drank it by the faint light of an old tallowpocked candle, as Jasper did not wish to light the lamp.

He took his warm coat and thick scarf, found gloves and a stout stick, and whistled to the dog. Skim, warm by the dying fire and not used to having his night's sleep interrupted, was as reluctant to leave as his master, but was at last persuaded to rouse himself and follow the men out into the chilly night.

'It's a fool's errand,' Jasper grumbled as the wind bit its way into his bones.

He said no more. It was a tidy stretch to the trapped hounds, and he was an old man. To-night, trying in vain to keep up with the Huntsman's tireless walk and Ned Foley's more limber legs, Jasper knew that his days were beginning to be numbered. The thought chilled him even more than the frost, and he brooded disconsolately as he watched Skim brighten and settle down to track the inviting smells that lingered on the heather.

Who would take an old dog? Jasper wondered. Perhaps Mrs. Jones. She at least seemed to understand what it was like to be old. Old, Jasper thought, and his mind flickered across the years. Eighty-six years. When he was a boy there had been none of this nonsense with motorcars and atom bombs, with television sets and aeroplanes that sent men flying across the world in the time it took to milk sixty cows. Come to that, they milked the cows in less time than it once took to bring them home from the pastures.

It was an unkind world, this world where so many men were rich and here on the fells they were still poor, grubbing a living out of soil that scarcely clothed the rock. Living on a pittance given by the Government. Grateful for someone to stand you half a pint or a fill of tobacco.

Skim started a small rabbit from a bush and chased it. Jasper whistled him back, and he came reluctantly, his bright eyes asking to be sent off again. Jasper would have carried him, but a stitch was cutting his side in two and his breath came uneasily, racking his chest and throat with pain. His legs ached, and he thought bitterly that it was not right to drag an old man and an old dog out for these young, never-care twopences.

1878, I was born, he thought. 1878. History-book times to these young know-nothings. Ask a boy to-day who was Dickens and he'd stare at you. Never heard of penny dreadfuls or of penny plain and twopence coloured and no idea what hokey pokey was. He could feel the icy edgy tang of it sharp on his tongue and hear the yell of

Hokey Pokey. Penny a lump.

Their modern, newfangled smooth-as-silk icecream couldn't touch it for flavour.

Other things you couldn't touch either, like the soft glow of gaslights on the shadowy streets, or the sight of the Manor House ladies setting off for a ball, in long dresses that trailed on the ground, their faces excited, eyes bright with laughter. Much more graceful, the women then. Not like these girls in trousers that walked on the hills, some of them in shorts so brief and tight that Jasper was often shocked. Large lumps of ham, he thought disapprovingly. He liked his women well hidden,

64

shy and veiled and mysterious.

Somehow it was easier to remember the past. Yesterday seemed far away, but the long years rolled back so that he could remember, with immediate freshness, the feel of the Armistice night celebrations in 1918, the terriers that had preceded Skim and now lay buried on the moor just beyond his wall. The old dog seemed to sense his master's thoughts, for he prodded Jasper's ankle with a loving nose, and followed obediently at heel.

The waiting men were huddled into their clothes, beating arms against chests to bring warmth. The moon had set, and the night was lit by stars, brilliant in the frosty air. Clumped trees were sharply etched against the midnight sky, and frost had outlined the grass with silver. Jasper and Ned and the Huntsman were part of the darkness, moving slowly towards them.

Jim Turner had a half-bottle of brandy with him, brought for his hound. He saw Jasper's exhausted face, and overcome by unexpected pity, helped the old man to sit on a boulder, and gave him the bottle. Jasper drank sparingly, but the welcome warmth helped him. He waited a few minutes, and then his age slipped away, and he looked with an expert eye at the country round him.

'This is where Button went down after the badger,' he said, and the Huntsman nodded. That had been twenty years before, but he remembered Button, a merry little creature with more humour than sense. The terrier had met a badger and taken hold, but been shaken free, and landed with a thud against a tree. Picking himself up, he shook his head, and took hold again. It had been a long fight without a victory. The badger retreated steadily, fighting all the way, and the men took the terrier and let the wild beast go, respecting his courage.

'There's an exit from a drain,' Jasper said, remembering. He stood up, his legs stiff, and walked over the tump. The men followed, their hounds leashed. Skim sniffed fox, and yelped and wagged his tail. An answering bay sounded from the ground almost beneath their feet.

'The fox will have left by the drain. Wonder why the hounds didn't follow?' Jasper moved on thoughtfully, and the question was answered.

'Landslip,' the Huntsman said. 'How deep?'

Ned had a spade and was driving it into the soil.

'Quicker to excavate than rely on the terrier from the other end,' he said. Earth flew, and Flier, thinking they were playing a game, began to dig frantically. Soil flew into his master's face, and Ned slapped the animal hard and swore.

'Let me.'

Jim took the spade. His thoughts were with Bella, trapped underground in a dark maze. She hated dark confined spaces. He had had to bring her out of the kennel he made, as it sent her wild. He wondered how she was faring, down there, away from the comfort of human touch and voice. The thought lent him urgency, so that within a few minutes his spade hit the drain with a hefty clonk.

Jo Appleyard took over. His thoughts, too, had been underground and he realised that, much as Madam irritated him, his affection for her was strong. He thought of the way she pressed herself against him when he went to let her out in the morning, of her small body begging eagerly as he cut up her food. He remembered the warmth of her tongue as she thanked him for her meals, and her absurd games with the cat and the old rooster that she drove almost to distraction.

Skim saw the drain opening, and looked up at his master with bright questioning eyes. It was familiar, and old as he was, there was a thrill of excitement in the contemplation of the dark hole.

'Find them. Find Bella. Find Madam.'

Skim was gone. A wriggle and a shake and his eager, fringed tail vanished into the gloom. There was nothing to do but wait. Jasper leaned his back against a sloping tree, a favourite hiding-place for the foxes. They could climb it easily and use it as a look-out post. At times men had passed beneath them, unaware of the sprawled red body looking down.

The Huntsman fumbled for his pouch and, finding it missing, sucked irritably at an empty pipe. Jo Appleyard offered him a fill and he made a lengthy business of crumbling the tobacco, tamping it into the bowl, and lighting it, his head sheltered by a looming rock.

Ned Thatcher smoked a cigarette and stared morosely at Flier, who was crouched, nose on paws, eyes watching his master. He knew better than to disobey. Ned revenged himself violently on an unruly animal. His thoughts wandered to his home, and his pretty, flighty wife. No harm in her, but a worry to a man. She never did as she was told, either, and laughed at his tempers.

Jamie Leigh crouched on his haunches beside Swiftsure, warming his hands on the animal's back. He was a reasonable man, and he trained his hounds so that they obeyed instantly, never needing a goad or a check. The Huntsman knew that Jamie's beasts were reliable and usually headed the Pack.

Jo Appleyard paced across the tump, noting the old runs. In places the tunnels were close to the surface and small outcrops of earth showed where they lay. He knew that here and elsewhere on the fells the badgers had fortresses that stretched for vast distances. Once a terrier had been lost for over a week, disappearing down an earth at the far end of Horton Pike, and reappearing from a small cavern close to the rocky scree

67

at the end of the mere. It was thin and exhausted, but had kept alive on water, and after a few feeds was little worse for its adventure.

'Rather be down there meself than sitting here waiting,' Ned said suddenly, pausing to listen. 'Keep hearing the oddest sounds.'

'Owls down by the water,' Jim Turner answered. He was used to waiting. Waiting for the plants in his nursery garden to grow, for tomatoes to ripen, for customers to pay bills. His wife scolded him for his patience.

'Let anyone make a fool of you, you will,' she often said in exasperation. 'Ask him for his money. He won't bite.'

Jim preferred to wait. He could not bluster or threaten and his little blue eyes had a habit of watering suddenly when faced with an awkward customer. It embarrassed him. It was easier to avoid making a fuss.

'The whole darned lot of them have got lost now,' Jo exploded suddenly. 'That terrier of yours has probably dropped dead inside the drain. I said he was too old.'

Jasper stared at him, his face stricken.

CHAPTER NINE

THE men did not know it, but trouble had walked into the earth at one end as Skim entered at the other. The terrier found Bella and Madam crouched, shivering and whimpering in the dark. They greeted him ecstatically, with licks and shrill whimpers that were too faint to be heard by the watchers above. Skim bore them patiently. He was about to turn and lead them out, when he caught the intrusive scent of an approaching badger.

He stiffened. Legs rigid, hair raised, he waited, a deep growl startling the hounds. A second later they, too, caught the scent. The three of them turned to face the newcomer.

He was a seasoned old boar, with a temper that was worse than that of many badgers. He hated dogs, and he put his head down, bulldozing forwards in a rush that would have bowled Madam stern over head if there had been room. Madam retreated. She had never seen a badger before, and she was very young and wanted company of her own kind before attacking such a fierce stranger.

Bella growled threateningly, more from alarm than courage, and backed away. The boar put his striped head low and advanced through the tunnel. The men heard Skim's excited yelp as he flew in to bite. His teeth were old and no longer sharp, and the badger shook himself, so that the terrier fell away, snarling and annoyed at his own deficiency.

The men stared at each other.

The badger attacked again. His brutal snarls drowned Madam's bay and Bella's growl. The terrier yelped, and got a firm grip on a paw. Painter, hearing Madam, pulled himself suddenly from Jo Needler's grasp, and flew into the tunnel, his music sounding above the din.

Jasper stared numbly at the open drain. His thoughts were with his terrier. He could visualise, only too plainly, the mêlée in the narrow tunnel, the biting savage head, and the old, almost defenceless dog. He shouted, but his voice was drowned by a new fury of sound from the ground beneath them.

The badger, penned in the dark, was caught by Painter's onrush. The hound snapped viciously, biting at muzzle and ear and paw. The badger began to retreat, first slowly, and then with increasing speed, backing towards a place at which he could turn and run.

The Huntsman, years of experience behind him, was following the sounds. He halloaed, guessing the badger was in flight, and anxious to call back the hounds before they were injured. The beast, now backing swiftly, thrust his head forwards, and gave a last savage snap.

His teeth met in the terrier's throat.

Painter bit again. The teeth loosed their grip and the old warrior shambled away into the depths of the earth, so that he could lie up and lick his wounds. The smell of him clung to the earth and the air, and the hounds sniffed and snarled uneasily.

Jo shouted to Painter. Reluctantly, the hound ran along the tunnel and out of the mouth of the drain. The watchers gave a deep sigh of relief as Madam followed, with Bella almost on top of her. The pair found their masters and, with paws on shoulders, licked faces, giving little whimpers of ecstasy, sterns wagging frenziedly. They were filthy with dark earth, draggled, and almost unrecognisable, lemon and tan and white overlaid with grime, but neither showed signs of wear. Jim Turner grinned at Jo Appleyard as he submitted to Madam's loving onslaught.

The Huntsman, who possessed an inner sense of his own that seemed to function like a clock, had his eyes on Jasper. The old man was crouched at the end of the drain, whistling to Skim. His face was greyer than the sky revealed by the first bitter gleams of dawn, his eye hopeless.

The Huntsman put a hand on his shoulder and crouched down too. Only then did he hear the sounds of laboured breathing and tiny whimpers as the old terrier dragged himself along, trying to reach his master before death claimed him. Waiting was unbearable, and there was nothing they could do. A spade at this point would only produce another landslide.

The badger's teeth had almost, but not quite, missed the terrier's jugular vein. The throat wound was deep, with a tiny nick in the big vessel which bled freely. The old dog became possessed with purpose. He needed his master's gentle hands. He knew that Jasper could help him. His strength was almost gone, but his will carried him along the last yards of the tunnel, almost flat on his belly, dragging himself over the uneven stony soil by pulling on his paws. The encompassing darkness was frightening. The badger might return. A puppyhood need for love and comfort was all that was left to Skim, and from it he drew unbelievable resources.

By now the hounds were quiet, Bella and Madam lying exhausted, glad to pillow their heads on their masters' shoes, thankful for fresh air that they drew deep into their lungs in satisfying gulps. Painter lay beside Madam, licking her muzzle, marking her for his own. She put her head companionably on his shoulder, and with a deep sigh, fell asleep.

Jim was about to offer the men a nip from the brandy bottle, as the hound had no need of it, when he saw Jasper and the Huntsman crouching at the tunnel entrance and realised Skim was still inside. He glanced at the others, and they followed his look, and then stared at each other helplessly. The agonising breathing of the old terrier was now clearly audible.

The harsh light revealed the long slope of the fells towards a distant clump of dwarfed trees, thick bramble coverts where the foxes hid, the sharp etched line of a drystone wall bisecting the distance, and below, half hidden by trees, the smoking chimneys of Tanner's farm. A man, dwarfed by the height, trudged out to bring the cows in for milking.

Beyond the farm the slope fell away to the mere, where rocks lay tumbled on the shore, and a line of dark trees edged the far away bare hill. A thread of foaming water slid down the rock face. A heron flew low, and landed, waiting for fish. There was silence, broken only by the desolate call of the curlew and the appalling sounds of the old dog's struggle towards safety.

Jim went towards Jasper with the brandy bottle,

looked at the old man, and shuddered as the Huntsman shook his head. There was nothing to be done or said. He went back to his companions, who were avoiding one another's eyes, standing unhappily as they watched the day grow brighter in spite of the flocking clouds. The hounds were listening too, and they stared at the men with puzzled unhappy eyes, as if able to sense the terrier's distress.

Skim had to stop and rest, but determination pulled him on again within minutes. He saw the outline of light at the end of the tunnel and almost stood. Jasper whistled softly again. The old terrier moved forwards, legs stiff, eyes glazing. He could just see his master's familiar and well-loved face. He pushed himself on, and was within reach of the entrance when his legs collapsed, and he lay, exhausted, whimpering faintly.

Jasper was, by now, flat on the ground, long arms reaching into the drain. His hands met round the old dog's body and gently, trying desperately not to add to the harm, he pulled the terrier towards him, shocked by the fragile feel of bones beneath the skin and the wet sticky blood that had matted on harsh fur. He could not speak when at last he brought Skim into the light, and stared at the gaping wound in the dog's throat as the terrier licked his hand.

Skim had found his sanctuary. Firm arms held him. With a little sigh the last breath went from his body. Jasper was left holding his dog, staring into the grey dawn, across the fells and up to the black rocks that echoed his desolation.

Without a word, he stood, rising stiff-legged, the terrier held tight in his arms. He did not look at the men. Swiftsure thumped his tail as Jasper passed. The men moved away, and let him through, unable to say anything to him. The old man did not notice them.

Set-faced, he walked back to his own home, carrying Skim gently, aware of nothing but that he had yet another hole to dig on the fells beyond his drystone wall, and another little mound to add to the graves of those terriers already buried there.

Ned Foley turned, his face anxious. The Huntsman put out a restraining hand.

'Let him alone,' he said softly.

A car breasted the distant hill, its horn sounding as a sheep strayed across the road. It was almost time to start work.

They whistled to the hounds. Painter and Madam. Flier, Bella, Swiftsure. The five rose eagerly, and followed

obediently, faintly puzzled by their masters' sombre expressions. Ned, watching Jasper's rigid back as the old man plunged blindly down the hill, felt in his pocket, and was rewarded by an irritated nip from the otter cub, who was hungry.

The Huntsman, following behind them, thought of his own past dogs and sighed deeply. He sighed again, knowing that for Jasper, life would never be the same. He did not think the old man, at eighty-six, would have the heart to rear another pup. He did not see Rusty run across the hillside, his mind for once busy with other thoughts.

Jasper saw the fox, and remembered Skim's excitement when he caught the old familiar smell. He began to remember other things. When he reached the cottage he was too unhappy to find a spade. He sat in the creaking wicker chair by the dead fire, the terrier's body on his knee.

There Ned Foley found him when he came at lunchtime, and it was he who broke the earth beyond the wall and took the lifeless body and covered it with gentle hands.

CHAPTER TEN

NED lit the fire and made some soup, and stood over
Jasper while he ate. He could not stay, and was glad
when the Huntsman came, bringing tobacco. He left
the two old men sitting in silence before a blazing fire,
the kitchen wreathed with smoke.

He climbed the hill, busy with his own thoughts. He
had seen the vixen in the night, and a lifelong need to be
friends with all animals drove him on, even though he
suspected that his efforts would be useless. Few men
understood that for Ned, the world of the wild creatures
was more real and far more necessary than the trappings
of civilisation.

When he killed, he killed cleanly, and for food. He
hated traps, and whenever possible removed their
occupants, so that there was constant war between him
and Brook Holler, who aimed to keep his farm free from
vermin by trapping the beasts. Brook was a sullen,

brutish man who detested the Hunt, and kept it off his land, threatening hounds and Huntsman with his old twelve-bore if they came near.

Ned found the vixen lying where he had seen her the night before. Her lacerated paw had opened again and he could see the pus running from it. She was too weary to lick the wound, and as he approached, managed only a token snap and snarl.

The youngsters were asleep, coiled together at the back of the cave. Ned, approaching cat-footed, watching the wind, had neither been heard nor smelt, and their mother's snarl was so weak that it did not wake them. He lifted her, and put her in a sack, leaving her head free, relying on her weakness to save him from her teeth.

She was terrified, but unable to struggle. Her eyes watched every movement as he carried her down the hill, and laid her gently on a pile of sacks on the floor of his small cart. He whistled his pony, an elderly little creature condemned by a farmer on the far side of Horton, and sold to Ned for the price of a week's help with the haymaking. He treated it gently, walking on steep places, and bought it all the food that he could afford, often working against his will to earn the money.

He found Dai Evans just leaving his surgery. Dai was a hot-tempered little Welshman who loved animals more than he did people, a trait that found him disfavour with the owners of pampered poodles and miniature pekingese. He lectured on the dignity of the dog and the need to treat him as an animal and not a mentally-deficient child, and bored women, with more money and time on their hands than sense in their heads, found themselves another Vet who did not thrust his own opinions on them and rouse faint feelings of guilt and uneasiness.

Farmers needing a man who would treat an animal and not badger for his fee, found him willing and devoted. He had spent all one night saving the life of a Siamese cat that had unwittingly eaten poison. He had his own methods of delivering awkward calves, and an unerring instinct for disease so that often he could diagnose where less dedicated men were baffled.

His own home was uncomfortably filled with animals of all sorts, for he had been fortunate enough to find a wife who had spent eight years working in a zoo where she was given all the sick and abandoned babies to rear. Farmers sent her ailing lambs, sickly pups, and even weakly piglets. Kittens sent to be put down invariably found a home, and stray dogs, a lame goat, a trapped badger, and an abandoned fawn lived in the barns and outhouses and scampered on the lawns inside the high brick wall of the vast old house that Dai had bought for the price of a modern car, its last owner having died and left the place a shambles.

Sheila Evans made a habitable flat on the ground floor, and turned the barns into a home for her animals. In one of them she boarded cats in luxury quarters that people fought to buy for their pets during their summer holidays. A second was a hospital where animals recovering from operations were kept warm by an old coke furnace, housed on straw or in baskets lined with old woollens according to their kind, and watched over with a loving devotion, extended to them by both Dai and Sheila and their four noisy children, who inherited their parents' interests in full measure.

Ned knew well that Dai would not refuse him help, and knew, too, that a fee would be waived in return for a few hours of wood-chopping or gardening among Sheila's roses.

He was right.

Dai looked at the fox, now lying on his operating table, her chest rising and falling with faint shallow breaths.

'I ought to put her down. Doubt if anything will help,' he said, staring unhappily at the wild wary face.

Sheila, coming into the room with an injured kitten in her arms, put the animal gently into a wire cage padded with clean newspaper and came to look.

'Don't put her down,' she said. 'Please, Dai.'

Her husband pushed his thick dark hair out of his eyes and grinned at her.

'Last-ditch Sheila,' he said in his soft Welsh lilt, but the words were not blame, they were praise. Ned heaved a deep sigh as the Vet filled a syringe with penicillin solution, lifted the fox, and caged her so that she could not move at all, being too closely confined. Before she realised what had happened, he sank the needle through the cage into her thick furry ruff. He drew his hand away smoothly as she tried to bring her teeth round to attack.

'Have to give her an anaesthetic for the next one,' Dai said. 'If that works, that is. I can't keep her. Are you going to cope now?'

'Of course he is,' Sheila said, and smiled at the man. He might be ragged and dirty and live in squalor, but he shared her intense need to bring help to animals, and no one could convince her that he was in any way undesirable.

Ned took the vixen, promising to bring her back next day, and Sheila found him a stout cage that would hold her, and put her inside on a deep layer of straw. Too weak to complain or struggle, the vixen curled up with her brush over her nose, and went to sleep.

'Feed her on rabbit, not meat,' Dai told him. 'Beg for chicken giblets. She might take rats too.'

Ned nodded. Sheila offered him coffee, and Dai brought him an old but decent shirt and almost respectable pullover and made him put them on. He showed them the otter, and then, seated at the kitchen table, eating Sheila's mouthwatering scones, he told them about the trapped hounds, and old Skim's death.

'Poor Jasper.' Sheila was quick with sympathy. Each death among her own animals was a deep personal loss, a betrayal of her trust, and she never grew used to it. She knew how much the old man had idolised his terrier, bringing Skim once through deep snow for an injection, even though he had had to struggle through drifts for a distance of over five miles.

Ned was thoughtful as he jogged home. He went inside his tiny hut, which would have surprised many people with its cleanness, for the floor was swept and the walls were whitewashed and his bed was neat as an army roll. He put the cage on the floor, put milk on a cracked saucer inside it, and left, taking the hungry otter with him.

He found Jasper once more alone, staring into the fire. An untouched cup of tea was on the table beside him, and when he looked up at Ned, his eyes were dark with pain. Ned was not sure whether he could reach through the grief, but he tried.

'Jasper,' he said. 'I need help.'

Jasper stared at him blankly.

'Found the old vixen. You remember, the one with the injured paw?'

Jasper nodded. Skim had run from her, frightened for the first time in his life, unable to understand his own reactions.

'She's sick. I've got her caged, and the Vet's helping. Can't manage to mind two animals. Can you take the otter cub?'

Jasper stared.

Ned shrugged, and then determined suddenly to give the old man no choice. He put the cub on the floor on the hearthrug, and went out, slamming the door behind him. Jasper sat, and brooded into the flames.

The otter had not been fed. Moreover, he was friendly, used to company and inquisitive. He was extremely hungry. He nosed around the floor, small, impetuous, and energetic. The terrier's drinking bowl was beneath the sink, still filled with water.

The cub understood water. It was his element, part of his familiar world. He dragged the bowl out with his teeth, so that the enamel made a familiar rattling noise that sent the blood to Jasper's face in absurd expectation. He saw the otter and sank back into his chair.

A moment later he turned his head as the little creature took a run from the other side of mat and landed in the water, so that it showered up the walls, on to the rug, and into a delectible pool on the floor. He rolled in the pool, soaking his coat, while Jasper watched, a faint interest stirring. He tried to remember the cub's name, but it eluded him. Its merry, whiskered face grinned up at him as it soaked in its puddle.

The game began to pall and did not satisfy hunger. The cub rolled across the floor, leaving trails of wet behind him, and before Jasper quite realised what was happening, it clawed its way to his lap and sat, soaking him, and gazed up with hopeful brown eyes, into his face.

When Jasper still did not seem to understand, the cub took hold of a gnarled old finger and began to suck. He sucked fiercely, his eyes appealing, and at last he was understood. A faint smile disturbed Jasper's mouth, and he lifted the cub, holding its warm body against him for a second, deriving comfort from the life and strength pulsing through it.

He found milk and put it, not into Skim's bowl, which he put away, as too sharp a reminder, but into a small bowl that had belonged to another terrier. The cub lapped eagerly, splashing drops all round, sending flecks of milk on to its fur, so that it was snowsplashed. It drank noisily, without inhibitions, and Jasper was unable to retain his deep gloom, as the little creature was so absurd.

He paused, wondering what to give an otter, but his choice was limited to sardines or the tinned meat that Skim had shared with Stalker. He opened the tin, wondering what had happened to the cat. He had not seen the ginger Tom all day.

Ned had not often found fish for the cub, and he, too, fed it on tinned cat food, so that the small beast took what was offered to him eagerly, eating it with as much gusto as he had shown when drinking.

Satisfied at last, he wandered back to the hearth-rug. Jasper had mopped the floor, and was back in his wicker chair, puffing at his pipe, when his guest came to him and demanded imperiously that he be nursed. The old man stooped and lifted the rough-haired body, and at that moment Stalker jumped through the kitchen ventilator window which was just big enough to allow him entry.

The cub lifted his lips in a snarl and Stalker hunched his back in astonished fury. Spitting, he sidled round the room, eyes on the intruder. The cub retreated into the darkness beneath the old man's jacket. It had not met a cat before, and this one was gigantic, ginger fur fluffed into an outsize mat, thick bushy tail erect, and eyes vicious.

Jasper sat helpless, not knowing what to do. Stalker and Skim had been together for almost the whole of twelve years, and the cat had grown set in his ways. The old man did not think he would ever make friends with such an unlikely newcomer. He was baffled, as he did not know where to put the otter, and did not want to send the cat away.

When the Huntsman arrived, anxious, a few minutes later, he found that Jasper was very busy. The otter cub was shut into the dresser drawer, which was open enough to allow a small inquisitive nose to poke out anxiously, while the old man held the angry cat and tried to smooth the bristling fur.

By the time the Huntsman went, a couple of hours later, an uneasy truce had been declared. The cub was asleep, and Stalker had gone to curl up on his master's bed and wait for him to come, as the night was cold, and the cat knew he would find warmth and company.

Jasper had been too busy to notice the way the cat had prowled about the cottage, and the Huntsman was thankful. He knew Stalker was puzzled by the absence of his lifelong companion and he hoped very much that the intrusive and boistrous cub might keep both the cat and his master from fretting.

CHAPTER ELEVEN

THE vixen began to improve. Dai cleaned the foot under
anaesthetic and dressed the injury. Penicillin began to
clear the infection and within a week she was feeding
greedily, taking all that Ned could bring in the way of
rabbits and chicken giblets that he begged from everyone with whom he had contact.

She did not trust him. He dropped food through the
top of the cage, avoiding snapping jaws, and she snarled
threateningly whenever he approached, although hunger always overcame her reluctance to touch the food
he had handled. Dai, calling in one day on his way
to Wellan's farm, looked at the vixen speculatively and
thought that she could soon be freed. She could stand

on the healing paw. Within a few days, it would have recovered completely.

Ned had no wish to keep her in a cage, and was anxious to have his otter back. The little beast had worked its miracle, and Jasper derived entertainment from it, but found that it caused too much work. It had no liking for tidiness and order, and slid through the cottage, scattering things, pulling the rugs adrift, or skidding along on them gaily, menacing Jasper's own safety.

The cub climbed the chairs and dived on to the table, helping himself to any milk he had not spilt. He rifled the waste-bin, dragged covers from the bed, destroyed newspaper, and chewed Jasper's slippers to soggy pulp. Stalker detested him, and spat furiously whenever the cub was near. The cat no longer came into the house, but was fed in the shed, and slept there, becoming surly, and on two occasions scratching Jasper, miserable with jealousy.

Dai hoped he had a cure outside in his station wagon. He left Ned, who was hoping to release the vixen at the end of the following week, visited Wellan's farm where he inspected a footsore mare, and found, to both his own and Ted's sorrow, that she had navicular, with no hope of a cure. Sadly, he arranged to put her down at a later date. There was nothing that anyone could do.

He drove on, and found Jasper shaking his head over a sea of milk on the doorstep, the cub having discovered the bottles newly left by the milkman. His batting paw had broken them, and to-day he and Stalker would both go short. Jasper grinned when he saw the Vet.

'He's a scamp and no mistake,' he said. 'I'll be glad when Ned lets the vixen go, and yet, don't know why, I'll miss him.'

His eyes strayed to Skim's empty basket, now chewed and monopolised by the little otter.

'I came to see you about that,' Dai said. 'I'm in a spot, and want you to help me.'

Jasper raised a shaggy eyebrow.

'Look.'

Dai led the way outside. A red setter was lying in the back of the station wagon, her nose on her paws. She lifted her head and stared at Jasper with sorrowful eyes.

'Her master's gone to jail. For ten years, and she is almost eight. He lived alone. If we don't find her a home she'll be put down, and nobody seems to want her. Don't like her history, though why the misdeeds of the master should reflect on the dog I don't know. We can't take her. You know what a houseful Sheila has already, and this time I've put my foot down. Only the kids keep crying.'

Jasper looked at the dog and she looked back and wagged her tail slowly, glad to be noticed. She was bewildered by the loss of her master, who had treated her well. She was far from home, and although Dai had been good to her, she found no place in his household. She had been alone, and with him she was one dog among many.

'She's gentle and quiet and taught to mind her manners when cats are about,' Dai said with a quick grin at Stalker, who was sitting on the wall busily washing under his tail and pretending that people did not exist. He flicked his fingers.

The setter jumped on to the driver's seat and out through the open door. She looked up at Jasper. He felt the silky hair on her head, and she thumped her tail again, watching him.

'Good girl,' the old man said.

The tail flicked again. Regally, she walked towards the open cottage door, and went inside. The two men followed, watching her as she nosed around. The cub whickered and retreated under a chair. She dropped on to the hearthrug, in front of the fire, looking as if she had lived there all her life, and the otter cub, curious, crept out to sniff at her. She licked his face, and covered him with a heavy paw, holding him still. He was so astonished that he did not move, and when she had finished he curled against her silky side and fell asleep.

'She did that with our kittens,' Dai said. 'Funny thing. She's been mated eight times, but never had pups.'

Stalker marched in, tail erect. He stared. He was used to dogs, and had always slept with the terrier. He gave the setter one bored glance, decided the otter was safely asleep, and jumped on to the old dresser, where he curled up and went to sleep.

Jasper looked at Dai.

'Her name's Nell,' the Vet said. He rubbed the dog's nose. 'Sheila gets dog-meat cheap. Come down and get it from us. I'll tell her to buy extra. If you can't come, send a message and Mark will bring it up and walk the setter for you.'

He whistled to the setter. She looked up at him, and turned her head away, seeking Jasper.

'Let her stay.' The old man looked down at her. 'I couldn't live without animals about the place.' He grinned. 'Always did have a way with dogs.'

Dai went, satisfied. He left a parcel of dog-meat on the table.

Jasper opened it, found that it was ready cooked, and blessed Sheila Evans. He cut it up, and the setter ate half of it gratefully, just to show willing, but Sheila had fed her well and it was not yet time for her evening meal. The otter investigated the plate, and finished

87

the meat eagerly. Stalker watched the setter. Jasper knew the cat was missing his old companion and hoped the two animals would make friends.

That evening he shut the otter in the cage that Ned Foley had brought him, knowing only too well what havoc would result if it were left free. At first it whickered indignantly, pushing against the wire mesh. Finally, it resigned itself and curled up, nose in tail, its back pointedly towards Jasper.

The old man whistled to Nell, who came obediently, and for the first time since Skim's death, went down the hill to the *Black Swan*.

The kitchen-cum-bar was crowded, hazy with blue smoke from strong tobacco, and ripe with the smell of wet coats and wet dogs, for it had rained heavily half an hour before. Jasper was aware of watching eyes that woke to startled interest as the setter trod delicately at his heels, ignoring the younger hounds. She settled at his feet, her rust-coloured body shining against his grey-trousered leg, and lifted her head and looked calmly at the men who were examining her, noting her points, and curious about her origin, for she was obviously no pup.

Jasper, aware of the curiosity, took his drink, and Mrs. Jones bent and stroked the setter, who accepted homage as if it were owed to her. She blinked once, gave a token thump of her plumed tail, and settled her head on her paws, eyes watchful.

The men had been feeling guilty about Skim. Had the hounds not strayed, had the Huntsman and Ned Foley not pleaded for the terrier, Skim would still be alive. They knew, too, that Jasper had taken the old dog's death hard. Relief made them voluble. Jasper found himself included in the conversations, overwhelmed with questions, offered half a rabbit, more than he could drink or than Mrs. Jones would allow him to have, while Nell was the centre of considerable speculation which he quelled by saying her master had had to leave home and go abroad for a long time.

When he pulled himself out of his creaking chair, and the setter, with a look at his face, waited to go, Jim Turner came over to him, and looked up into his face, blue eyes watering.

'I wanted to thank you,' Jim said awkwardly. 'Sorry . . . About Skim. Never thought . . . Glad you've got another dog,' he ended, not having given expression to his thoughts at all.

Jasper put a hand down and the setter's muzzle came into it at once. She was as much in need of affection as he.

'Don't worry,' Jasper said, suddenly glad to be accepted again, and aware that his feud with the men who hunted had died as absurdly as it had started. 'Poor Skim was old. Better to go quickly like that than to ail and have to him put down. Been afraid I'd go first and leave him. Nobody would want an old dog. This one . . . She's young, and anybody would take her on.'

'You're good for your century, Jasper,' the Huntsman said, coming into the room in time to hear the end of this statement. 'I'd have taken Skim. You know that, you old fool. You'll be here for that telegram from the Queen, yet. First in the village to get it. You can't cheat us of that.'

'Been planning your birthday cake,' the baker said, a froth of foam on his beard.

'I'll walk up the hill and stretch my legs a bit. Take a couple of bottles with us, Mrs. Jones.' The Huntsman grinned at her.

Nell followed them out into the frosty dark. When

they reached the cottage she took her place on the hearthrug as if it were her right, and Stalker, who was already curled up before the dying flames, looked up at her, and did not move. She put out her paw and licked him as she had the otter, and with a deep sigh the cat came to lie against a new companion, knowing that she had come to take Skim's place.

CHAPTER TWELVE

RUSTY was lying up on a bink, where the sun could warm him as it filtered through the covering bushes. He was half asleep, his ears alert for sounds, his busy nose working, taking up the scent of a distant bonfire, the smell of damp earth a few feet from where he lay, the sharp keen feeling of frosty grass, a rank whiff of stoat that remained from the night before, and the tantalising reek of rabbit, safe in a nearby burrow.

A second later he was alert, head lifted, eyes searching, ears pricked for the distant song of the hounds. They were running in full cry along his brother's trail, and a second later Rusty saw Rufus break across a field, twist through a flock of running, bleating sheep and drop into the dry ditch to double back and merge with the fox-coloured dying bracken that lined the edge of the field. The running fox and baying hounds sent

Rusty's heart thud-thudding, a deep excitement mounting through him. He controlled it. His mother had taught him well, and he knew what kind of game he was going to play.

He could see the hounds spread over the fells. Behind them, tireless and watchful, was the Huntsman, the men pressing him close. Above, slipping through the lanes, glasses ready, excitedly asking who had seen the fox, and where was the Pack, came the car followers, eager to see as much as they could of the chase without expending any energy. Ford and Austin, Vauxhall and Triumph, they followed one another in low gear, or made occasional dashes to another view-point, as the hounds took the scent and followed it farther afield. With them were a few lads on bicycles, and behind them came the children, Susan Wellan following determinedly on Vicky, her pet donkey.

It was an odd day, the kind the weather forecasters call dull with bright periods. Clouds raced in front of a vicious, biting wind that nipped noses and toes and fingers, and teased the hounds, as it froze damp earth, making it treacherous for running pads. The Huntsman knew that if the wind dropped, as had been forecast, there would be mist. He knew he must watch. Mist on the fells on an icy night was no joke, and most of the foot followers were older men, with a few women. The youngsters did not come, or chose the comfort of cars.

Jasper heard the view halloa, and came out into his garden, Nell following him closely. Having lost one master, she had no intention of letting this one out of her sight. She slept beside Jasper's bed, occasionally rousing in the night and standing above him to make sure he was there. He had caught her several times, and each time had petted and fussed her, knowing that she felt desolation as keenly as he mourned for Skim.

Now, as he watched the Hunt moving out for the first time since Skim had died he remembered how the old dog had come running at the sound of the hounds and the music of the horn, and how eager he had been to join in. Jasper was glad that he no longer had to tie the terrier up. There had been reproach and misery in the raisin-brown eyes whenever Skim had been chained, and the old dog could never understand why he was not allowed to follow the Hunt.

Nell, sensing his withdrawal, thrust her nose against his knee, and pushed, reminding him of her presence. The distant sounds meant nothing to her, although she was interested, as her moving ears showed, and her bright eyes watched as the little figures strung themselves out over the moor.

It was very cold. Jasper put on his coat and muffler, pulled an old cap well down over his ears, found gloves, and whistled to Nell. If the fox broke up towards Buttonskille, as seemed probable from the way the hounds were running, he might see something of the Hunt, and also give the setter some exercise. She was so well-trained that she followed meekly at heel, waiting for his command before she crossed the road. He wondered about the man who had brought her up, drilling her to such obedience, and yet been able to commit a crime that would jail him for ten years.

Rufus was tiring. He slipped on a rocky scree, scrambling up the slope towards a narrow gully where water should mask his scent. When he reached it, he found solid ice, and hesitated, not sure of his next move. Before he could decide, Rusty sprang from above him, crossed his trail, showed himself in full view, and pelted downhill at a tangent, with the wind smoothing his fur as he ran.

Rufus ducked into hiding behind a small cairn and crouched, panting. The hounds saw the second fox and turned, all except Painter, who followed the original trail, but was called back by the Huntsman who decided that the second fox might give them a better run over easier ground. Madam, chasing madly over wet ground, failed to see an icy puddle and skidded wildly, landing on her chin with an air of pained surprise. Painter passed her, his tongue lolling in a grin that made the Huntsman wonder if the hound was in fact laughing.

Swiftsure was running easily in the lead, nose down again, but scarcely needing the trail, for the wind sent back the rank fox scent, and the pack ran eagerly. Bella stopped to nose Madam, and the little bitch picked herself up and ran on a few paces, but stopped, puzzled, and licked at her paw. The Huntsman caught her up in a swift movement and bent over her. He glanced down at the ground. A piece of sharp glass glinted in the sun, and a blood-trail marked where Madam had run. He signalled to Jo Appleyard, who swore, and lifted his hound.

'Nasty gash,' the Huntsman said, his eyes watching the hounds. 'Get it stitched. Bad luck.'

Jo turned and thumped across the fell towards the road, his heavy boots ringing on the hard ground. Blood poured from the gash and Madam whimpered. Jo soothed her roughly, his hand stroking her coat. He climbed the wall and reached the lane level with the largest car he had ever seen in his life, which was making a fair job of turning in a space meant for a bicycle.

He waited.

The turn completed, the driver opened the door.

'Bad luck,' he said, in an unfamiliar accent. 'Like me to drive you to the dog doctor?'

Jo stared.

He looked down, saw the blood that stained his clothes, and nodded.

'Thanks.'

The driver, a wild-haired man with a bronzed face and narrow moustache, dressed in rough tweeds, thrust his hand through his hair and let the car into gear with a jerk that sent them bouncing a few yards along the lane.

'Glass?' he asked.

Jo, overwhelmed by the magnificent car, nodded. The driver handed him a box of paper tissues, and he tried to stem the flow of blood by holding a thick pad of them over the injury. Madam sat quietly. She was always gentle and very co-operative when she was sick or hurt.

'I'm from the States,' the man said. 'Name of Hinney. Came to see if there were any of my folk left in these parts.'

'There's Rob Hinney. He's cowman at Wellan's.' Jo answered. The name made the man seem more familiar, and he vouchsafed his own.

'Can't make your Hunt out,' Hinney went on. 'Read up all about hunting in the Lakes before I came over. Knew it wasn't done on horses. Where are the Horton Kennels?'

'Horton Kennels?' Jo laughed. 'We don't have a kennels here. Can't afford it. Just a case of each man keeping his own beast and putting them out to hunt as a pack. It works quite well.'

'You have a Huntsman. I thought he ran the kennels.'

'Our Huntsman's retired. Used to be over at Lime-cast, but they got a young man in. Found the work a bit much. He can still hunt a pack though, and he knows all about hounds. We just do it for fun, mister, and a few side bets. And to keep the foxes down.'

He pointed to Dai's big old house.

'Won't be off with the Hunt?' asked Hinney.

'Not him.'

Jo climbed out, holding Madam.

'Thanks, mister.'

The big car sailed back to the fells as Jo went to find Dai and get Madam's injury stitched.

By the time Hinney found the other cars, Rusty had run through thick heather, dropped down a steep over-hang through planted conifers, pelted over loose scree, and taken shelter among Wellan's cows. The Jerseys ran, lowing noisily, desperately afraid of the stranger in their midst.

The fox doubled through them, dived into the ditch, breeched the hedge, and started off again between high walls towards the main road. Swiftsure and Painter ran neck and neck, Swiftsure dropped behind for a second as Painter soared over the wall, but touching down a second later the pair were only a hundred yards behind the racing fox.

Bella was next, landing delicately, and her master, seeing her from a viewpoint on top of the wall, almost lost his footing in excitement. Jasper and Nell came round the corner and stood back as Wayward, Flier, and Tangent leaped, losing only seconds before they regained their balance, and bolted after the leaders, followed closely by Tanner's two pups, Walker and Runner, while the other youngsters straggled after them. Last of all, fully a hundred yards behind the others, came Terror, his master, Wellan, grinning whole-heartedly because the pup did not seem to have the faintest idea of what he was doing.

'Glad to see you, Jasper,' Wellan said, and smiled as Nell stepped protectively in front of her new master. 'That's a fine bitch. Bit of a change from old Skim.'

'Just as well,' Jasper answered. 'Doesn't remind me of the old dog's ways.'

'Skim was a grand terrier,' Wellan said. He grinned broadly again. 'Seen my pup? He hasn't a clue.'

Terror was following behind the other hounds, his head up, his stern wagging, in contrast to the head-down, concentrated attitude of the more experienced beasts.

'He's hopeless,' Wellan said. 'Kids have spoiled him.'

'He's young,' Jasper answered, his eyes on Painter, who was obviously following the drag. 'Time'll cure him. Look at that!'

Painter was marking and gave tongue. The youngster lifted his head, eyes eager, and, suddenly aware of his own business, pelted forward to join the racing pack. The Huntsman came striding down the lane, his eyes on the hounds, making for the busy main road at the corner.

Rusty pulled himself out of the ditch by the roadside, and eyed the traffic thoughtfully. On the breast of the hill was a large lorry, carrying cement, and behind it, caught and unable to pass because of heavy opposing traffic, was a covey of cars.

The fox waited, listening to the hounds' clear cries as they nosed towards him. Swiftsure had found the ditch and was struggling out of it when his quarry sped across the road, narrowly missing death under the wheels of a big tanker.

As the hound reached the roadside the fox made safety and the traffic, now able to overtake, sped past. The Huntsman, putting on a spurt that caught at his chest, almost winding him, managed to shout the hounds to keep back, and they waited, eager and obedient until he called them on again, thankful that none had been lost under the speeding wheels.

When the road was clear the hounds bounded over, questing eagerly. A boy pointed to the ditch, marking where the fox had crossed, and the Huntsman signed to Painter to take up the scent. The big hound cast, puzzled, running in a circle that baffled the man until he reached the ditch edge and saw that it was stained with horse manure through which the fox had run.

With the hounds checked, the Hunt caught up, the footsloggers eating their sandwiches as they walked, anxious to miss nothing. The hounds waited, nosing out their owners, asking for patting and petting and the Huntsman went among them with his encouraging voice, rubbing behind an ear here, patting a neck there, watching for signs of jealousy and giving Flier a bite of biscuit when he knew the hound's master was not looking. Flier had a rough time at home.

A few minutes later the fox broke cover higher on the fells, coming into view for a second, running strongly. Wayward, using his eyes instead of his nose, gave tongue and rushed forward, and a moment later Painter found the line and began to follow it, the other hounds at his heels. Above them, in a narrow lane, the sun reflected on the windscreens of waiting cars, and on binoculars fastened on the field.

Rusty angled away, dived through bracken, tore into brambles, leaving tussocks of red fur on the thorns, found a hollow oak, and slipped through the arch it made, coming headlong on to sliding scree. The Huntsman saw him, but did not call to the hounds. He preferred them to mark out their own scent. He spoke gently, his low voice sending encouragement. He kept the horn for rare moments, relying on his personality to keep his pack in order.

Above him the fox doubled on its trail, and thoughtfully put its head inside a drain. The rough coat caught on brambles that marked the entrance, and then, without going in, Rusty turned, trod through leaves that covered a layer of ice, and slipped into a gully which led back to the line that Rufus had taken. A few minutes later the brothers were together, crouched on a well-covered bink, looking down on the hounds marking the empty drain. The terriers went in, and drew a blank. Grumbling, the Hunt turned away.

Rufus was fresh, and it amused him to show himself. A yell of view halloa from down the valley sent the pack skidding towards him, and he leaped away, bounding eagerly towards the straggling village street. The hounds were tiring and followed far back. Rusty dropped wearily into denser cover, curled up, and fell asleep, remaining alert for any sound, so that a chattering bird made him raise one eye-lid sleepily, and each cry from the distant hounds caused him to lift his head.

Rufus trotted gaily down the village street, well aware that the scent of man was far stronger than his own. Painter, surprisingly fresh, was the first hound to follow, with Swiftsure running a close second. Bella had stopped to drink, and was trotting wearily, while the others were dropping out, one by one, and far behind Ted Wellan was tracing Terror who had found a false trail and was following it doggedly up on to the fells again.

Bess Logan heard the two hounds cry, and looked from her window. The fox was making for her garden. The old woman set her lips. She hated the Hunt, and all her sympathy lay with the quarry. She found a pile of gravel, and stood beside it, leaving her cottage door ajar. Rufus, hearing Painter give tongue a bare twenty yards behind, slipped through the crack. Bess cackled and shut the door. The fox was safe.

The hounds reached her and eyed her, unable to understand her menacing shouts. They knew where their quarry lay, and wanted it. They told her so with tongue and ears and head and stern, and the Huntsman came up to find Bess, a tiny, determined, grey-haired, hump-backed woman with a nose that met her chin and little brown eyes that glinted hatred, brandishing a stone at his best hound.

'Bess,' he called. 'Let be.'

'Come any nearer and I'll throw at you,' Bess offered, her small mouth grim.

The men were straggling along the streets, their boots ringing on the cobbles of Buttonskille. It had been a long day, and they were tired and inclined to anger.

'Let the hounds take the beast,' Ned Thatcher shouted.

'Get out,' Bess answered. She flung the stone she was holding. 'Get out.'

Swiftsure, receiving the pebble on his shoulder, whim-pered with pain, and Jamie Leigh was quick to go to his hound, and reassure him. He faced Bess.

'Fling your stones at us, not the beasts,' he said; 'they're only doing their duty.'

'I'll fling them at the lot of you,' Bess cried. She held up her door-key. 'I'll drop it in the well before I let any of you by.'

The Huntsman collected the pack, and fussed them, praising them for the day's work. The men took their own hounds, and turned towards the *Swan* and the Hunt teas, while women and children trudged home, to mend fires and brew tea, and talk over the day's doings.

Bess went into her kitchen. The fox was crouched by the back door. He eyed her anxiously, ears erect. She flung him a portion of the rabbit she had been saving for her dinner next day, and went out, leaving him to eat. She left him alone until dark, and then let him go, watched him slipping into the bushes behind her cottage, and away up the fell.

He found Rusty, and a moment later a yelp excited them. Ned Foley had released the vixen, her foot completely healed. The three of them greeted each other with yaps of joy, with nips and yelps and teasing games, and then curled up as they had when the youngsters were cubs, three bodies curled together, happy in reunion. They did not start the night's hunting until the moon was high over the peaks, silvering Hortonmere with magical light.

CHAPTER THIRTEEN

WHEN Jasper took Nell into the *Swan* he found an air of excitement. To his astonishment, tea had been put aside for him, and Jim Turner said sheepishly:

'We meant to tell you, Jasper. There's a place laid as long as you want it.'

Jasper's eyes gleamed. He could think of nothing to say, and he knew Jim was trying to make up to him for the loss of the terrier. He did not speak, but bent down and patted Bella's head. She licked his hand. Nell butted him in the knees, jealously, and when he sat to eat, stayed beside him, her head on his knee, daring any other animal to come near.

A moment later the excitement was explained, for Rob Hinney came into the room.

'Hey, Rob,' Jo Appleyard shouted. 'Here's your rich cousin from America come to look you up.'

Rob stared in astonishment at the stranger, but was prevented from saying anything by Jo, who went on to add his thanks for the lift that afternoon and exhibit Madam, her foreleg bandaged.

'Six stitches,' he said proudly, and added 'Picnickers! Not the sense they were born with. Breaking glass all over the fells.'

'You're Rob Hinney?' the stranger said.

Rob nodded.

'Ever hear of your great-uncle Silas?'

'Aye,' Rob said. He rubbed his thatch of red-grey hair. 'Me granddad's brother Silas, that would be. Went to America.'

'He's my grandfather. So we're cousins. Come on, landlady, drinks for everyone. Let's drink to my English cousins.'

'You live in America?' Rob asked, somewhat overcome by his new-found relative.

'Near Pittsburgh. Big industrial city. Work, myself, in industry as a matter of fact. Came over on business and thought I'd try and look the old home up.'

'Glad you did,' Rob said. 'Perhaps you'd like to come and meet the wife? We still live in the old cottage that Great Uncle Silas was born in.'

The stranger was visibly impressed.

'You like England?' the Huntsman asked.

'It's a great little country. I like your old villages. There's history there. I like your roses, too,' he added. 'Never seen such roses.'

'Don't you grow roses in America?' asked Mrs. Jones, moving the kittens out of the way as she carried glasses of foaming beer across to the table.

'No, Ma'am. My wife wanted some. So I dug a trench. Dug it deep and wide and filled it with everything that roses like. And with roses. Hundreds of dollars' worth of roses. And the rose beetle walked right in. You get that over here?'

Heads were shaken.

'Waal, we do. And I got right there hundreds of dollars' worth of the most expensive sticks you ever saw in your life. So I dug them up and planted dahlias,' he added philosophically. 'You grow dahlias too, but it's your roses I go for.'

It was not easy to talk to strangers, especially sophisticated Americans, and the silence that followed these remarks became both lengthy and uneasy as men who are used to talking only of country matters tried to think of a topic that might interest a foreigner.

'That's a fine dog you have, Mister,' Jack Hinney said to Jasper, who patted Nell on the head, and roused himself from a stupor caused by Mrs. Jones' outsize tea, coupled with the warmth of the fire and a glass more beer than he was used to.

'Had her long?' the American added.

Jasper's brown face creased into a grin.

'About a week,' he said.

'A week? She's not a young dog.'

'No,' Jasper said. He had no intention of revealing that her master was in jail. He fondled her long silky ears, and she gazed up at him lovingly.

'A beautiful animal. Know anyone with a pup for sale? One of those fell hounds of yours. Never seen anything like the way they work on a trail. I'd like to take one back with me.'

'I can let you have a pup, Mister,' Jim Turner said. He owned a second bitch, Meggie, and she had recently whelped.

'She's a sister to Bella here,' he said, forgetting that the stranger would not know what he was talking about.

'Bella's a good hound, Mister,' the Huntsman said.

'Her sister is as good. They're sturdy pups.'

'I go home next week. Will they be ready?'

'They will. Ten weeks old by then.'

'How much?'

'How much?' Jim stared. They did not buy and sell pups on the fells but exchanged them for goods, for a couple of sacks of potatoes, or a help-out with winter hay, for a supply of lettuce or tomatoes, or eggs for the winter.

'Ninety dollars?'

The Huntsman did a rapid conversion. Near on thirty pounds.

'That's too much, Mister,' he said. 'We wouldn't want to cheat you. The pups must be worth about ten pounds apiece, that's about thirty dollars.'

'At that I'd be cheating you,' Jack Hinney said in astonishment. 'They fetch good prices back home. I'll pay you sixty dollars for a dog hound.'

Jim was unable to believe his ears. He stared at the American as if afraid he would vanish into the ground, but the wild-haired man remained good and solid, and sat drinking as if that amount of money meant as little to him as a cup of tea, and only the Huntsman realised that to the stranger such a sum meant very little, whereas to Jim it represented a fortune.

Next day Jack Hinney chose his pup, with the Huntsman guiding him, although it was soon obvious that he had little need of help, for he went with an unerring eye to the strongest and handsomest dog in the litter, a tan and yellow and white hound that Jim had named Ravager because of his habit of tearing anything within reach.

'He'll need a lot of training, Mister. Hounds come wild when young,' the Huntsman said.

'He'll learn. No, sirree,' he said sharply as the little

animal leaped to worry a hogskin glove, and the pup stopped at once, recognising authority when he heard it. The Huntsman gave one of his rare smiles. He knew the pup would be in good hands and well taught.

Jack Hinney spent his week well, visiting Wellan's little manor farm, and being rewarded with a visit from the ghost, which locked the bathroom door good and truly before he went to wash his hands, so that both Wellan and Rob had to force the door open, and prove to their guest that the hinges were oiled and the lock was free and there was no known reason for the door to jam.

He went out with the Huntsman and the pack on a training walk, watching with interest as the hounds were called back, or sent foraging, were held together, or dispersed over the field, all by a casual gesture or a word. Bella put up a rabbit, but the Huntsman called her off and she came at once, and was rewarded by a biscuit.

Jack Hinney took tea with his cousin, and Rob's wife made him a spread equal to any that Mrs. Jones could put out, while the children, dressed in their best and unnaturally quiet and clean, listened with awe to this stranger from halfway over the world as he told them of skyscrapers, and the Statue of Liberty, and the great factories in Pittsburgh, and the snow in winter—though that they could understand, for often the village was cut off by storms and snow that lay for days.

The American admired the old china ornaments that stood on the shelf.

'Useless ugly things,' Margaret Hinney said, vexed. 'Collect the dust. But they were left to us by our grandmother.'

'They'd fetch a fortune in the States,' their cousin told them.

Rob stared at him with disbelief.

'Haven't you tried to sell them, if you don't want them?'

'Who'd buy those old things?' Margaret asked.

'I would. We'll go to Kendal and get them valued. Don't want to cheat you. How about it, Rob?'

Rob laughed, and that night told his wife he thought the American was crazy, but he called a very different tune when, on his day off, they went to Kendal and the old china was valued at a sum that made him stare.

'Reckon we've all come into luck this winter,' Rob

said as he toted the churns next morning, with Tom Ladyburn helping.

'Ah,' Tom said, his mind on his own small nest-egg. 'If we'd killed a fox that first Hunt I'd have no money in the kitty now. Reckon that pair of foxes is lucky.'

'So do I,' Rob answered, for if Madam had not cut her leg chasing the pair of them, the stranger would not have offered Jo a lift and might have passed by without finding another Hinney. It was only chance that made him stop and watch the Hunt that afternoon, for he had known only that his grandfather came from somewhere in the district and was quite unaware that he actually hailed from Horton.

A sudden skurry from a flock of crows on the hill made both men turn and look. The two foxes, red brushes flying, were coming home from hunting. They were glimpsed briefly and then were gone.

'And the best of luck to the pair of them,' Rob said suddenly, and with great good will as he lifted the last churn on to the table beside the road, where it waited for the lorry to pick it up.

CHAPTER FOURTEEN

WINTER set the ground harder than granite, killed the foraging, so disposing of the rabbits, and the foxes took to haunting the mere, where often an unwary duck or heron had its feet frozen into the water. No one could remember such weather, and heads were shaken as snow fell on hard ground, and hunting had to stop, as the hounds could not move through deep snow that lay soft and thick in the high places.

Foraging was hard for the foxes, who found the going bad. They began to haunt the hen runs, and more than once a shot startled the night, driving them farther afield where men and dogs were less wakeful.

The vixen was so hungry that she fought Bess Logan's old Tom, who marked her for life with a deep scrape across the corner of her eye, and returned to his mistress with a torn ear to match his other ear, tattered long ago by a rival Tom, probably Stalker.

Hortonmere froze so solid that the village boys skated and played football, ducks and herons found thin feeding, froze, and died, and fed the foxes. The villagers found deer raiding the sheds, pushing doors open in a search for stored turnips and potatoes, and three hinds found fat feeding on Wellan's farm, where they leaped into a field and took the hay, and remained, unmolested, until the thaw came, as Wellan had plenty of feeding stuff and no desire to drive them away.

For the first time for many years the farmers brought the sheep down from the hills, penning them in fields close to the houses where their feed could be supplemented, and later replaced, by hay. Land-Rovers and Austin Gypsies combed the fells, bringing down ewes that had strayed too far, while the busy sheepdogs hunted diligently, nosing their charges out of drifts where they sheltered from the frequent storms that raged fiercely on the hills.

Nell, her new master discovered, had a good nose, and several times found sheep that had dropped into ditches against the high stone walls, seeking to bury themselves away from winds that bit through woolly fleeces, while often soaking them so that the wool froze, causing the animal much suffering.

Lambing became an unusual ordeal. Foxes travelled from over the fells at the scent of the afterbirths thrown by the shepherds beyond the hedges. The farmers became more careful, and all traces were removed and burnt, for the sake of the new lambs. Night after night torches and lamps gleamed in the fields as the men made the rounds, and brought in any ewes they could find, so that lambing took place in the big barns, where hay formed a barricade around the walls against the cold.

Wellan's farming methods showed proud results, for

in all that bitter winter he lost only two ewes and one lamb of his flock of over three hundred. Tom Ladyburn was the shepherd, and he had marked each ewe with the date of her lamb, long ago, when the rams were with the flock.

The big barns were cleared, and the new mothers brought inside. Weak lambs went at once into the big annexe to the kitchen where the boiler kept the place warm, and Mrs. Wellan and the girls kept bottles ready for any time of day or night. Any Wellan to be seen at that time had two bottles of warm milk tucked into a pocket, ready to give at once to any lamb that seemed to be in trouble.

Ted Wellan and Tom worked the night through in shifts, four hours on, four off, patrolling the flock, singling out the lambing ewes, helping this one, taking that to the Vet for a Caesarian, removing one of a pair of twins, and ever keeping a wary eye for foxes. A coke brazier near the field gate gave warmth that was very necessary for frozen hands, and the kettle was kept boiling continuously on the Aga in the kitchen. During the day Mrs. Wellan took over, while the men slept. She was as good with the stock as any of them.

Jasper came down to help feed the orphans, bringing Nell, who spent her time ranging the fields and barking whenever a fox came near. Ned Foley came too, glad of warmth and comfort for once, and slept on the barn floor on a pile of hay, ready to call out if any of the sheep were in trouble.

Meanwhile the foxes ranged, always on the watch for ailing lambs. They found several bodies at Tanner's farm, and took them, leaving Tanner trying to protest that they had killed the lambs themselves, although his shepherd was well aware that they had died of neglect, having been born out in the fields and frozen before the ewe could warm them.

Late one February night Jasper brought coffee out to Tom Ladyburn, who was trying to help a ewe with twins while keeping his eye on another that he suspected would need operation to remove her lamb. The twins safely delivered, he put them with the mother in the big barn, where she bedded herself at once on warm straw and licked them clean. Tom removed all traces of the birth, and took his coffee, warming his hands on the cup.

'Listen!'

Tom cocked his head, as Jasper called his attention to Nell, who, head on one side, eyes bright, was listening to some distant sound. It came again, a far away keening cry that made the sheepdog's ruff bristle, and bared both dogs' teeth in a snarl. Behind, in the shed which kennelled them, Wellan's hounds whimpered.

Moonlight flooded the fells, outlining tree and peak and the slow rise of the hills black against a sky in which the stars scintillated with unusual brilliance. Down the distant hill, black against the snow, fled two foxes, and behind them, in a stream of darkness, pelted a mass of little animals.

'What on . . . ?' Tom was startled, and Jasper gave a thin whistle.

'Weasels packing,' he said. 'Never hoped to see . . .'

The ewe that Tom was watching struggled to her feet, and the lamb dropped unexpectedly, but the effort was too much for her, and Tom put her body outside the field, intending to deal with it later. He wrapped the tiny newborn creature in his coat, and watched the animals for a moment before turning towards the kitchen where he knew Mrs. Wellan was sleeping on the settee, ready for whatever came in the night.

He left her with the lamb, and went back to find Jasper standing blowing into his hands, mesmerised, while Nell and Barney, the sheepdog, crouched at his heels, growling.

Rusty and Rufus had eluded hounds with ease, but this was different, and the pack behind them terrified them so that they fled with lifted ruffs and ears flat, running full out, downhill. They had been hunting through the wood, feeding on the bodies of frozen birds, when the weasels scented them, and blind instinct made the little killers congregate, so that they could hunt down their kill *en masse*.

Murder followed them, on dozens of tiny feet. Eyes glinted red in the night as the weasels rushed on, never forsaking the trail left by the bounding foxes. Breath rasped in Rusty's throat as he found a ditch and ran along it, pads slipping on rotting frozen leaves. Close behind him Rufus whimpered, the thick fur of his ruff erect with horror.

Small feet whispered along the ditch. The foxes raced among the startled cows, the herd scattering, lowing lustily. Rob Hinney heard the din and was on his feet, pulling on clothes as he ran to the field. He saw the fleeing cattle, and whistled as the weasel pack fled between stampeding hooves. The cows huddled in a corner, beneath the trees. The foxes leaped to the wall, slid down the embankment and were into the lane that led to the farmyard and the sheltering sheep.

The weasels came on. Ted Wellan's gun spoke, and a small body dropped into the snow. The foxes ignored the gun, and jumped on the hen-house roof, so that the startled and terrified birds added their clamour to that of sheep and cows. An owl swooped and took the dead weasel away to his hungry mate. They shared it greedily.

The weasels found the dead sheep that Tom had left

to bury later. Neither he nor Ted knew why their pursuit had stopped until dawn came, and they went to find the body. Instead they found only bones, and around it in the frozen snow, the mark of many tiny paws.

The foxes left the hen-house roof and crept into the stable, where they bedded in the straw. Boy Blue and Bracken were restless and uneasy, but no one knew why. Twice Ted went in to quiet them, unaware of the two brothers hiding in his hay. They paid for his hospitality by catching five rats that night, and on other nights the hounds called as the foxes slipped quietly into the barn, their forages remaining undiscovered.

On a later night the weasels ran a deer to death and killed it beyond the top of Hortonmere, while the vixen cowered in a stony gully, afraid that the wind might change and the little monsters scent her.

By now she had joined her sons on their rat-hunting expeditions round the farms and hen-houses, and between fox and owl the vermin were diminished. The countryfolk put it down to the hard winter, and never guessed why.

CHAPTER FIFTEEN

THE thaw brought the snow from the fells, filled the
rivers and brooks, and flooded Hortonmere. Frost came
again and froze the floodlands, enclosing tree and bush
and rock in an icy grip. The water raced in foaming
masses down the screes, rivers changed their beds, and
Wellan's found itself isolated by fields of water.

As the first flood waters crept over the grass Ted
Wellan, Rob Hinney, and Tom Ladyburn, with anyone free to help, drove the stock on to higher ground.
Mrs. Jones lent her two big unused barns for the ewes
and lambs, and Tom spent the few hours left driving
the tractor, towing the hay-cart, so that there should be
food for the flock.

Jasper, high on the hilltop, found himself giving hospitality to the Hinney family, as Uncle Silas's cottage
was up to the eaves in icy flood water. Ned Foley offered

his help to the men operating the rescue boats, and was first in and last out when there was dangerous work to be done.

There was no thought of hunting. The hounds were taken to the vicarage, and lodged on straw in a deserted crypt, the Huntsman moving in with them, as his own home was under water. He slept on a camp bed, warm beneath a mound of blankets, as the old heating system grumbled into life and the big stove warmed a place that had not been used since the last floods, a quarter of a century before.

By day he helped the cooks peel potatoes and make soup, and developed an unexpected talent for keeping restive children quiet with hunting tales and songs, so that often the old Sunday schoolroom echoed, not with prayers, but with yells of 'Hark halloa' and the soft wail of 'Gone away', which woke the hounds kennelled below to frenzy.

Wellan's family moved into the vicarage, but Tom Ladyburn, an exile from his own home stayed in the house with Ted, sleeping upstairs, where they cooked camping meals on a primus in the bedroom. In between times they visited the flocks, using a boat for transport to dry land, checked on the Jersey herd, which Rob Hinney was guarding in a small field next door to Bess Logan's little house, and made unhappy lists of fowls lost in the encroaching water.

The view from the windows was astonishing. A scene of field and moor and hill was replaced by a flat steely expanse of grey, out of which the hills reared bleak heads, cloud-capped. Rain fell, as if there was not enough water over the land. Otters swam beneath the windows, swans floated down the village street, ducks brooded where once had been roses and dahlias, bobbing at their own reflection and diving repeatedly and uselessly for vegetation which was too far down to find. The villagers flung them breadcrumbs, holiday-minded children leaning gaily from upstairs windows, delighted by the scene which so appalled their parents.

The foxes lay up on the peaks, away from the water, and away also from any but the most meagre food. Once Rusty tried swimming for duck, but the current from the inrushing water was so strong in the mere that he was lucky to be swept ashore again. He stood, shaking with cold, terrified by the unseen strength that had challenged his own, and returned forlornly, empty-handed, to lie up beside his brother.

The sheltering hinds swam to safety. Ted watched them go, glad to think that they had escaped death in the water. Later that day a struggling foal came down on the current, battling bravely. The windows at Wellan's were large, and as the little beast came by, Ted and Tom pulled him to safety, and dried him by the fire.

When the boat came at midday with hot food and blankets and a pile of groceries, Ted asked for hay, which they brought from the top of the stack, and the two men bedded the foal in a corner of the big bedroom, shifting furniture to give it stable room. It soon dawned on Tom that it was too young for the only food with which they could provide it, so they diluted their milk and gave it to the foal to suck from a rag, a slow and messy business.

Later that day Ben Legan from the stables came in a boat to fetch the foal, which had lost its footing and been washed away. The mare was alive and well and hankering for it. The men were not sorry to see it go. It was not easy to have such a companion inside a house.

When the water went down the village was busy.

Those who had been lucky enough to escape the floods helped those whose homes were ruined by them. Floors were scrubbed clean of layers of dark filth, carpets, already rotting, taken out to dry and later, burn. Furniture was salvaged, bedding dried, and relief vans drove through the slimy streets, bringing food and clothing and bedding.

The children splashed off to school, stamping through the muck in sturdy wellingtons. They went regretfully, wishing that they could stay and play in the streets, salvaging unlikely objects brought down by the water. Ned Foley went round with the squad that was disposing of bodies as sheep, cows, and hens floated down, and were left, bloated and unsavoury, when the waters receded.

The foxes found fat feeding as they followed the diminishing flood. Many of their familiar trails were unusable, blocked by swollen brooks through which the water surged, peaty dark, boiling over the rocks in a swirl that let nothing live in it.

Mrs. Jones kept open house and cooked meals at all hours of the day and night, charging a tiny sum for her labours, so that the exhausted women could have a break from scrubbing and washing, and come and find warmth by the fire and comfort in exchanging experiences over a cup of tea. She was almost empty at night, for there was much that the women could not do.

At Wellan's everybody turned to to try and make the house comfortable again. The bathroom door had been torn from its hinges, and as Tom replaced it he hoped that the flood would have drowned the ghost, and that the new door would not jam. The haunted barn had been washed away. Its battered planks had come ashore over a mile beyond Hortonmere, on the other side. Ned took the pieces for firewood.

An icy wind swept in from the hills, drying out the sodden fields. The stock was brought home. Slowly life began again, with grim reminders in the empty hen-houses, and the uncarpeted floors and gaps where some piece of furniture had had to be scrapped because the water had rendered it useless. The exhausted villagers settled down again. The hounds came home, and the Huntsman collected them and schooled them as a pack, encouraging them with shouts of 'yick' and 'coope'. No scent lay in the foiled fields. The smell of the rank flood slime was everywhere.

There came a day bright with springtime promise. Homes were shut and the villagers took to the fells, as the hounds followed the Huntsman, eager to go. Up on a grass-covered bink the vixen heard the familiar sounds and lifted her head. She was soon to whelp again. She had left her sons just before the flood and taken up with a big rangy dogfox from Coniston way. He had travelled miles to find a mate, and he nosed above her now, listening, ears cocked, eyes uneasy.

He nudged her. She followed docilely as he loped away from Hortonmere, and took her far over the fells, away from the villages, to an earth that was deep and safe and secret, and far from huntsman and hound. Here, within the week, she gave birth to four cubs, and here she stayed the whole summer, while the dogfox hunted for her, and once killed a questing stoat that threatened his young.

Neither of the brothers had found a mate. They were still together, both bachelors, as they had not moved away from home ground and no other foxes roamed that part of the fells. As the cry of the hounds echoed thinly from the hills, they were both off together, running strongly uphill so that from far below came a yell of 'View halloa', as one of the followers sighted them.

Painter fled after them, the pack behind. The going was bad. There was mire in the fields, bog from the floods, and hounds and men floundered badly, plodding through thick mud that clung to their boots, and betrayed some of them so that many a man was covered in muck when he went home that night.

The foxes, high on the rocky slopes, were never in danger. They hid at last in a cave that led off behind a small waterfall, creeping through a curtain of foam along a slippery ledge to reach sanctuary. Soon the Hunt was in such trouble that the foxes were forgotten.

Painter knew about ice. He had skidded upon Horton-mere joyously when the freeze was at it worst, and now he came to the frozen edge of the water, thick from the previous night's frost. Before anyone could check him he was running fast, trying to cut off the long spur that prevented him reaching the foxes. Behind him came the pack, Madam treading warily, Bella eagerly, Wayward coming blindly, bent on catching the leader.

The men, swearing as they blundered through sticky mud, yelled in unison. Painter checked. The ice gave way, and a second later he was deep in the mere, the current tugging him beneath another spur of ice. Bella and Wayward went in after him, but Madam managed to turn on her tracks and came whimpering back to her master. She shuddered as he stroked her and put his handkerchief through her collar to hold her. The rest of the pack returned, and were immediately seized and immobilised, while the Huntsman, Jim Turner, Jo Needler, and Charlie Dee hurried to the edge of the ice, trying to assess the situation.

Charlie whistled. Wayward turned his head, and made

a bold effort to climb on to the ice, but was defeated by the breaking edges. Painter was already being swept into the flood, and Bella, whimpering desperately, was struggling against the current.

'I'm going in,' Jim Turner said.

'Don't be a fool, man,' Charlie answered, his eyes on Wayward. 'You'll catch your death of cold, and do no good. The hounds'll have to take their chance.'

Jim whistled. Bella tried to turn and was swept towards the farther edge of the mere. The Huntsman walked along beside her, yelling encouragement, so that she kept on swimming, although she was almost exhausted. The Huntsman worked out that if the current took her, it would cast her ashore on a tiny spur. He walked on to the slippery rock and smashed the ice around it with a long pole, so that the bitch could come straight towards him. She saw him, and, as the shore came closer, swam more strongly, the pull of the water helping her.

By the time she reached the spur, Ned Foley and Ted Wellan were beside him, and Jim was at the edge of the water, almost demented with anxiety. Ready hands hauled Bella ashore, where she dropped, soaked, panting and shivering with cold.

Jim took off his scarf and rubbed her, while Ned helped, using his gloved hands, blue where they showed through the holes, to give the hound friction. She stopped shivering and shook herself.

'Take her home fast, Jim, lad,' the Huntsman said in his soft voice. 'Rub her down and give her some milk and brandy. She'll do fine. We can get along here.'

Jim set off briskly, and the others at once turned their attention to Painter and Wayward. Painter was almost under the surge from the fall that led off the sheer face at the far end of Hortonmere, while Jo floundered along the miry edge, trying to reach his pet. Wayward had found a spit of solid ice, and was trying wearily to pull himself on to it. It held his weight, but his paws could gain no grip and time after time he fell back into the water.

Jasper watched unhappily, Nell beside him. Suddenly the setter tore herself free from the old man's grasp, fled down the muddy path, and, before anyone could check her, ran out on to the icy spur. As Wayward struggled once more to free himself from the river, she crouched on the ice, paws straddled, her weight spread, and caught the young hound's scruff in her jaws.

She heaved, and with her added help, Wayward was out of the water, the pair of them sliding backwards. The Huntsman grabbed Nell's tail as she skidded sideways. She came towards him, her jaws still firm on Wayward's loose flesh. The three of them went over in the mud, a mass of flailing legs and tails and heads and licking tongues. The men pulled the three of them to their feet, and Nell found herself the centre of such pats and congratulations that she was bewildered, and freed herself so that she could run back to Jasper and stand in sanctuary, pressed against his legs, with his familiar hand on her shoulder, and his gentle voice soothing her.

The surge of water had sent Painter into the centre of the mere again. He was almost spent. He paddled feebly, the current tossing him backwards and forwards. Jo had given up hope, and stood dumbly watching, when one of the Tanner boys came pelting down the field, his feet sliding on mud. He held a length of rope at the end of which was fastened a slender block of wood.

'If we throw this, and Painter has the sense to grab

it, we might be able to drag him ashore,' Pete Tanner said eagerly.

He flung the coiled rope. The wood fell within inches of Painter's muzzle.

'Grab it, boy,' Jo shouted. 'Fetch it here.'

Brown eyes stared reproachfully, but Painter, always obedient, took the wood in his jaws. Hands seized the rope and began to pull. Painter felt the wood give, and tightened his grip. A moment later, he realised that he was being dragged through the water against the current, and he hung on gamely, his big teeth clenched to stand the strain.

When he reached shore, his jaws were bleeding, and the block was clenched so firmly that his teeth were embedded in it, and he had to be prised free, his stern wagging thankfully throughout the painful operation.

It was a weary and pitiful procession that went home that night, and the *Swan* lacked several familiar faces, as the men tended their half-drowned hounds. The Hunstman nursed a strained and aching back in his own cottage, where his Siamese cat, a present from his married daughter, purred, eyes crossed, glad to have her master at home.

Up on the lee of the hill the two foxes hunted for rabbits and then rested. Far away came the keening cry of a calling vixen. Two pairs of ears pricked, alert, two voices answered. The cry came again, followed swiftly by Rusty's yelp. Rufus turned on him, snarling and yelped his own reply.

When the moon changed Hortonmere to shimmering magic, the two brothers were alone, each one running his own trail towards the enticing song of the lone vixen.

CHAPTER SIXTEEN

THE calling vixen went to earth in a grassy bank beyond a swollen stream. Rusty and Rufus dared not swim to her, and they had not found a way to cross when snow began to fall. The blizzard came swiftly, out of a darkening night, and if they had not been preoccupied by the wild enticing screams, they would have seen the signs in the sky and wind and taken shelter.

There was nothing near. They had left the bracken-brown moor and dead heather tussocks far behind. Here there was only scree and mud and the roar of the racing water that tumbled over the banks to run skeltering down the hillside, filling the brook that led into Hortonmere.

Above them, edging along the wind, a lone hound hunted. He had escaped, weeks before, from a pack that was kennelled beyond Windermere, and now, lean-flanked, with outthrust ribs that showed through his gaunt body, he was tracking a hare. The scent was strong, and lay breast-high as he coursed alone towards the brothers.

Their scent came full and strong, startling him. He had not heard the calling vixen. He guessed that the foxes would be trailing his hare, and he was hungry. Moonlight glinted on his lemon-patched coat. Painter might have been his brother.

The falling snow almost blinded him. The scent of the hare vanished. The hare herself took full advantage of the stream and put long leaps between her and her enemy, fear giving her heels much greater impetus than usual.

The foxes caught the taint of hound. They did not know he was alone and almost starving. They only knew that here was an enemy, and with the memory of long days spent fleeing from the yells and the baying of the pack, they forgot their temporary difference, and were, once more, allies.

They moved together, dark shapes gliding through the falling snow. The hare, crouched in the lee of a boulder, almost buried by drifts that blew up towards her, scented them and shivered, but need not have feared, for they, too, were gripped by danger, and had no ears for her, nor did they catch the faint fugitive scent that lay on the ground she had covered.

The hound faltered. He had come from a bad kennels, where the food was meagre and the Huntsman indifferent to the needs of the Pack. A paid servant, with little love of tradition or hunting, he was a small man with a meagre mind, who beat the hounds when they disobeyed him. Ranger, the solitary, beaten by the man and bitten by his kennel-mates, had been glad to leave.

He had hunted alone for weeks, existing on small birds, a rabbit, and once a hare. He had not missed his kind, nor had heed of man, but to-night when the darkening wind brought thick snow, and his coat was sodden and his pads were frozen, he longed for warmth.

He did not scent the two brothers, lying low in the thick tangle of bramble that bordered the moor. He found their outward trail, when they hunted the vixen, and he floundered in deepening snow, looking for food, with half an eye open for man. Man, he knew, would give him shelter. Once during his lonely weeks, a shepherd had fed him, but the sheepdog, jealous, had chivied him away. He had a sore bite on his shoulder as memento of the fight.

The snow troubled him. It blocked his view. His pads sank into it, and soon it masked all scent. Once he stopped, panting, and lay with steaming breath, but the clamminess was hateful, and he rose again, shaking himself. He stopped to paw at his eyes and muzzle, shaking his head, bewildered by the drifting flakes that began to cover him.

Dawn, when it came, brought little brightness. Twice he floundered into the edge of a drift, but blundered out again, and trotted wearily downwards, looking for houses. Smoke from the whitened roofs blotted the sky, and he began to run. Sounds came from the village street. The muffled wheels of the milk-cart, the postman's tread, the paper boy's whistle.

The Huntsman had slept badly. Snow made the Siamese uneasy. It called to him in the night, and he let it into his bedroom, where it prowled restlessly, playing with the lace of his shoe, and pulling aside the curtains so that it could stare, bewitched, at the swirling flakes. When morning came, the shepherd from Wellan's came too, asking for help with the sheep and lambs that were buried in the late and unexpected snow.

Jasper was already out, Nell working a scent of her own that brought to light a ewe and late newborn lamb, the cord not yet severed. The shepherd dressed the cut end, and rubbed the lamb with tar, to discourage the attentions of foxes, who, he averred, would never touch an animal smelling so strange.

The Huntsman had no dog of his own. Once he had lived with a pack, and now he was reluctant to give his affection to one single animal, although he often wished that some twist of fate would force him to change his mind.

He watched Nell quartering the ground. Beyond her, three sheepdogs were busy, and he gave all his attention to the spade that was thrust into his hand as Chico barked his discovery in frantic excitement.

The ewe they uncovered had well-grown twins, and all were fit. One of the Wellan girls took a dog and herded them into the big barn, where the ewe found hay and began to feed greedily, while the lambs sucked from her, tails wagging in frenzy.

Ranger heard the barking dogs, and hesitated, but he was famished and he could smell food cooking. Chops slavering, he stumbled down the hillside towards the grouped men, his stern wagging. As he approached he gave a deep-toned cry that had no strength in it, and stopped, startled at his own feeble sound.

Only the Huntsman heard him, and he, turning his head, thought he was dreaming, for he thought he looked at Painter, grown skeletal overnight. He chucked in shocked horror, and the other men turned and stared at the gaunt creature that loped towards them, legs unsteady.

'Who in sanity would let a hound get to that state?' Ted Wellan asked.

Ranger looked from one to the other, hope lighting

his eyes and then dying. The wagging stern drooped. The bold head dropped. He did not know that the men were too shocked by his starved body to speak. He turned wearily, prepared to slink away to the moors.

The Huntsman was the first to recover. He snapped his fingers.

'Here, lad.'

Ranger lifted his head and the light came back to his eyes. He walked forward, and with one last effort, licked the outstretched hand. There was an angry murmur as the big hound dropped, exhausted, and lay, unable to lift his head.

Ted Wellan took the thin body in his arms and carried it to the kitchen, followed by the Huntsman, already remembering his kennel-lore. The farmer went back to the field, but the Huntsman supervised the preparation of warm milk laced with brandy, and fed it to the hound, talking gently, hands stroking the weary beast.

'What will happen to him?' Susan Wellan asked.

'I'll take him in and feed him up,' the Huntsman said, suddenly aware that his decision had been made for him. The Siamese would protest, but there was no reason why the two animals should not settle down together. It would be good to train his own hound again. He regretted the long past days when his word had been law in the Kennels. Money would not be easy. A hound needed meat and was costly to feed, but the farmers would help. There was often a still-born calf or a lain-over piglet, and the meat was good. In the old days, the Hunt Kennels had the right to all such dead animals in farming country, and the men knew how little he had to live on. He grinned wryly at the thought. Only the old age pension, and no secret about that, and the tiny pittance that was all the Hunt could allow to a retired servant.

Ranger was exhausted. He crawled to the big sheep-skin rug that lay in front of the roaring fire and slept. The Huntsman went back to the fields. A warm wind was already thawing the snow, so that the ground was slushy, the men working irritably with wet hands and boots through which water sometimes seeped. The weary sheep bleated, lost lambs cried out in panic, and it was no consolation to know that the scene was the same on every farm in the vicinity.

Tom Ladyburn swore as one of the dogs uncovered a frozen sheep, her newborn lamb dead at her feet. He set both aside to bury. When he looked again for them the lamb was gone, a trail left in the snow showing where Rusty had dragged it.

'Reckon he deserves it,' Ted said wearily, looking at the long track that led up the hill. 'Surprised he could drag it so far.'

'Funny the dogs didn't see him or scent him,' Tom answered.

'Probably did, but they knew they had to get on with the job.' Ted blew into his hands. It was time for a break, and there was soup and tea waiting. They counted the sheep. Only the dead were missing.

Inside, in the big kitchen, the floor muddy with many feet and wet with thawing snow from hefty boots, they found the stray hound eating greedily from a bowl containing meal soaked in broth. When he had finished, he thumped his tail, and looked hopefully at Mrs. Wellan. She gave him a plate full of rabbit meat, which he ate greedily.

'Eat like that and he'll soon be fat as butter,' Tom Ladyburn said, cupping his hands round the big mug of tea to warm them.

Outside the sky was patched with blue, the spring sun melting the snow so that it went as fast as it had

130

come, pouring off the fields into the ditches by run-offs that were so full and noisy that the ponies from the Riding Stables shied when they passed them.

Larks spiralled into the sky. A courting blackbird sang in the almond tree in the Wellans' garden, its plumage glossy and dark against the first faint pink blush of bloom. A child, going out to look for a last patch of snow, found that the snowdrops were in full flower, their hanging heads white against the new-washed green.

There was food for all who had helped at Wellan's. Nell followed Jasper up the hill. The Huntsman watched them go, and whistled the hound, who came eagerly. He was tired of being an outcast. Here was food and, better, kindness. Trustingly, he followed his new master home.

The Siamese retreated, a mass of fluffed fur and outraged bottle-brush tail, to the top of a high bookcase. The hound looked to the man for guidance.

'Sit. Good lad,' the soft voice said.

Ranger dropped obediently on to the hearthrug. He looked about the room, its low, whitewashed stone walls hung with trophies and pictures of past glories. Masks and brushes of long-killed foxes surrounded the low hearth. There were hunting prints on the walls, of the kind of Hunt the Huntsman had never known, where the gay-coated riders jumped their horses over ditches and fences and stake and bounds.

Ranger recognised the hunting horns. He knew the familiar calls, the 'halloa' and the wild excitement of the 'gone away' as the fox broke cover and tore off in full sight. He knew the sounds that heralded the end of the day, the exultation of the kill. He thumped his stern and the Huntsman grinned.

They settled for the evening, the man drawing on his long-stemmed pipe, the hound stretched at his feet, secure at last, feet twitching, stern moving softly, as he relived old chases in his dreams. Sung, the Siamese, came stealthily from the high cupboard, moving alertly, ready to bound back should his peace be threatened.

But the hound slept on. The cat leaped lightly to the high back of his master's leather chair, its sides patched and torn where the Siamese had stretched and sharpened wicked claws. No amount of chastising had ever cured him of the habit, nor had a rough log, placed beside the hearth taught him better manners.

He settled himself, one paw on the Huntsman's shoulder. The fire crackled. Outside the warm cottage a hunting owl called softly and mournfully. The cat stretched luxuriously, and climbed on to his master's shoulder, and then crawled on to his knee. Ranger lifted his head, and the cat spoke, warningly, dangerously. The head dropped back to the hearthrug, and the hound watched, eyes wide, as Sung began to wash, starting with one slender black paw and ending with an indecorous tussle at a piece of irritating fur between his hind legs.

The hound sighed deeply, stood, and put his head on the Huntsman's knee. The cat stopped washing and stared. Ears flattened, he began to swear, but stopped when the brown hand slid comfortingly over his dampened fur. He settled, drowsing, blue eyes half closed, basking in warmth from the fire, and the hound leaned his full weight against the Huntsman's legs.

Musing in the firelit room, the Huntsman thought of the coming summer. He would have to advertise the hound, but he guessed that it came from far away, and would not be missed. He would enjoy training it. He thought of names of past animals, and of the moors over which this one had ranged, so that the name Ranger came pat to his mind.

'Ranger,' he said.

A warm tongue licked his hand. Soon all three drowsed, and the clock ticked in the silent room, and the falling coals made soft sounds that were echoed by the cat's faint wheeze, the hound's soft snore, and the old man's deep breathing.

CHAPTER SEVENTEEN

The little vixen crossed the stream by a fallen tree. She
stalked a bird, and missed her kill. Brush lashing, she
went hungrily down the scree to the mere, where she
found a sitting duck, cradled above her eggs. The drake
saw her coming, and fatherhood made him bold. He
flew at her, quacking noisily.

The sound brought the other ducks off the water.
There was a whirr of wings, and the sudden terror as
a mass of drakes flew towards her, and an angry beak
tore at the soft flesh above one eye.

She fled, away from the water and the anger that
surrounded her. Long after she had gone the drakes
were still sounding their warning cries. The duck settled
more comfortably on her nest, her warm down incubat-
ing the new lives within the eggs. It needed only a few
days to hatching, and then she and her mate would be
endlessly busy, keeping their brood of ducklings safe

from fox and eagle and threatening wicked pike that lurked in the unseen deeps of Hortonmere.

The vixen was lonely. Her mother and brothers had both been killed by the Hunt of a far-away village. They deserved their fate, for all three were lazy hen-robbers, never looking for more difficult game. The farmers had been determined to put a stop to their depredations, and the hounds had chased them tirelessly, day after day, for over a fortnight before the last one was dead.

Left alone, the vixen moved away to look for company. She travelled miles, hunting as she went, and spent the days lying up in dead bracken or brittle heather. She crossed many roads, and several drivers saw her loping in front of them and into the hedgerow on an early morning drive, her fur speckled with dew. Others glimpsed her at night, a sleek shape running for cover, or crouched, terrified by headlights, at the edge of the road, her eyes reflecting redly.

Her scent lay on the moors, and maddened the two brothers, so that often now the fights over a kill were bitter, and Rufus had a torn ear, and Rusty a stiff shoulder where teeth had bitten deep. Soon they separated, no longer lying together for warmth at night and each hunted on his own, marking out his territory. Snarls greeted an intruder.

Jasper often saw Rusty, now heavy and muscular, his bushy brush black-tipped, as he climbed towards his den, a deserted badger earth on the sloping hillside. He and Stalker met often, but ignored each other. The cat found mice in plenty up on the hill and the fox did not threaten him. The rank scent made Nell bark, but she was too well trained to leave her master and hunt alone.

Rufus was determined to find the vixen first. He followed her trail by day and her scent by night, but she was cunning, and was not yet certain that she wished for his company. She knew how to foil her own scent, and often, while he searched for her, used tricks and wiles that baffled him completely. Once she lay above him, stretched against the rusty trunk of a beech tree, while the first fattening buds helped to mask her. She watched him lope past, but something about him made her hesitant and she did not reveal herself.

Rusty caught her scent and heard her call, but was busy hunting, and, although he cocked an ear, and turned viciously on his brother, he did not at first seek her out. Not until the full moon made him restless and he was sure of frequent meals of young rabbit, did he try and track her down.

His scent intrigued her, so that several times he glimpsed her, but she was too clever for him. She was young, and not yet ready to breed. She might choose a mate, but no cubs would be hers until the next year. She remained hidden and coy.

Hunting had ended. No more would the men bring the hounds to the Huntsman to train as a pack. The moor was silent, no longer echoing to the horn and cries of 'yick' and 'yoick' and 'coope'. The Huntsman walked his new hound and watched him working. Ranger was quick to the scent, eager to the trail and more than once followed the drag of the vixen. He would prove an asset when the winter came again.

It was good to have a hound, the Huntsman mused, as the two of them quartered the moors, watching for signs of fox and for new ways and paths that a clever beast might tread. There had been no kill all winter. The men were not perturbed, for once the old vixen had recovered her strength she and her sons had not raided the hen coops.

They had good sport, and an unusual winter. Looking

back, the Huntsman thought of the way in which the foxes were linked with the village life. Had there been no Hunt, Skim would be alive, or perhaps dead of old age in a gentler fashion. Yet Jasper was happy with Nell, and the winter had brought fortune to Ned Foley, who, after his help at the time of the floods, had been given a tied cottage on Wellan's farm and had settled down to a more reputable way of living, although he still brought rabbits for Ranger and only grinned when asked their provenance.

He marked the path that the vixen took, with next year's Hunts in mind. His legs did not cover the ground so fast. He wondered if any man would take over the pack when he was too old. Retired huntsmen were few. England was changing swiftly. There was less money to spare, and many of the famous Kennels were finding it hard to make enough each season to feed the hounds and to pay the huntsman and keep the animals healthy. Vet bills alone could amount to a tidy sum.

An unusual winter! Looking back, the Huntsman thought of Jasper, now happy with Nell. Of Tom Ladyburn, who thought that the foxes had brought him luck, and whose small nest-egg offered security for his old age, and enough to wed off the daughter who was to be married in the summer.

Ranger, following on Rusty's track along the road that led to Wellan's, gave tongue. The Huntsman called him back, and he came reluctantly. No one had ever claimed him and he was now a fine animal, and Painter's double. Like Painter, he promised to be swift to follow a trail, and courageous. Once, during the long summer walks, he drove off a weasel, which fled through the long grass with a painful nose. The Huntsman was well satisfied.

Rob Hinney met them as they took the short cut through the Jersey field, the hound well to heel, following obediently. He called a greeting and made a fuss of Ranger.

'Remember my American relation?' he asked, his wide mouth grinning. 'He wants a bitch from Horton, so that he can breed hounds. Won no end of prizes with that dog hound in America. Says he'll pay anything we like to ask for a good one.'

'Jo's breeding from Madam and Swiftsure,' the Huntsman said after a moment's thought. 'Should be good pups. What's he want to do with the hounds?'

'Show them. Breed them. Said he'd like a pack, but he might be joking. Funny sense of humour, they have over there,' Rob said, as if he were speaking of an alien planet. 'Sent us a small fortune for Mag's Staffordshire cow. Remember it? The ugly old thing!'

He laughed engagingly.

'Funny, if it weren't for them foxes, we'd never have met. Funny old life, isn't it?'

'How's the pup going to America?' the Huntsman asked, his mind on practical difficulties.

'Jack's coming over for it when hunting starts. Bringing his wife and two kids to see Uncle Silas's cottage and the way we live. Fair taken with it. Seems to find it queer.'

He turned as Ted shouted from the house.

The Huntsman leaned against the white five-barred gate and looked up the hill. The moors were soft with the green of unfurling bracken, patched among the brown dead fronds. New heather was sprouting. The ducklings were hatched on Hortonmere and their tiny bodies floated in file between the duck and the drake. He counted seven families before he tired.

The trees were fuzzy with unfurling leaves, their soft outlines furry and strokable. Beneath them bluebells blurred the ground in a haze of colour. Primroses starred the hedgerow along the lanes, and the tiny village girls worried their mothers by lingering long on the way home from school, filling their hands with flowers. Jasper, walking with Nell, was enchanted by them, and often one or other would stop and stroke the setter and proffer her primroses to the old man, who took them courteously, and put them in a jar on his kitchen table.

He woke one night to hear an eerie screaming almost outside his door. Nell was growling deep in her throat and Stalker was crouched on the foot of his bed, fur raised, ears flat, making the room hideous with his swearing yowl.

Jasper climbed out of bed and drew aside the curtain in time to see the vixen knock the lid from his dustbin. She foraged inside and came out with the carcase of a chicken that Mrs. Jones had given him, as most of it had been left after a wedding breakfast at the *Black Swan*.

As she turned away, Rusty came loping towards her, and behind him, like a shadow, came Rufus. She backed, her trophy held in her jaws. Rusty pranced towards her, head high, nose questing. She watched him, her eyes bright.

Rufus snarled. Rusty turned and his brother pounced. Nell and Stalker flew to the window, staring out at the twisting bodies that bit and tore in deadly earnest, while the little vixen, the cause of all the fuss, lay down at a safe distance and gnawed the carcase. Jasper grinned.

The moon was bright enough to see the end of the fight. Rufus fled, brush down, towards the hillside. Jasper saw him top the rise and vanish in the undergrowth. He would lie for a day to lick his wounds and then seek new hunting grounds, far away from Horton, where he might find himself a mate. From now on, he would be solitary.

Rusty walked towards the vixen. She snapped at him, afraid that he would steal her chicken. There was still flesh on the inside of the ribs, and her hunting had been unlucky. The dogfox lay down, waiting patiently for her to finish eating.

Stalker crouched stiffly, voicing his anger. Nell's growls were softer, but she obeyed her master and tried to be silent, although it was hard, with the rank wild smell of fox flooding in through the window, and the two animals there outside, in full view.

Jasper watched them until the vixen finished and licked her chops. The old man was curious. He had seen the beginning of the story and wished to know the end. Thanks to the foxes, Skim was dead, and he had a new dog. Life for many in the village had been changed. Now the story was about to take a new turn.

Rusty approached her closely. He rubbed his head against her neck, questioningly. He was no longer the victor, certain of himself. He was a suppliant asking for favours. She nipped him, in play, and took to the hill, fleeing up the rough ground as if she were possessed, Rusty after her.

'They'll stay together the summer, and breed next year,' Jasper said to Nell, who wagged her tail happily.

He felt wide awake. He lit the lamp and brewed a cup of tea. The cat asked for milk, fondling his thin ankles until he bent and filled the saucer, and gave Nell a biscuit from her box so that she would not be left out either. Sitting there, by the last glow of the dying fire, his thoughts followed the same path as the Huntsman's earlier in the day, as he thought of the changes the winter had brought, mostly small, but all affecting the life that he knew in the village.

Sleep did not come even when he was warm in bed. The cat settled beside him, the dog lay on the rug. Their even breathing was company. He heard the call of the vixen and the exultant yelp of the dogfox and smiled to himself in the dark. There would be more foxes on Horton Fells, and men with hounds would hunt them again, in spite of change in the world. English country folk had hunting in their blood and could not help themselves. Not for the sake of the kill, nor the hope of a death in the morning, but for the thrill as the hounds found the trail, the view, and the check, and the joy of watching as they worked out the path that the fox had taken, and of the wild chase that followed.

The yelp came again, its note triumphant.

Jasper smiled in the darkness, for he now knew the end of the story. The Huntsman turned in his own bed, the Siamese complaining, and Ranger lifting his head to listen to the sounds on the moor. The words of 'John Peel' ran through the old man's mind:

The sound of his horn brought me from my bed,
The cry of his hounds, which he ofttimes led,
For Peel's 'View Halloa' would awaken the dead,
Or the fox from his lair in the morning.

The old man slept, knowing that tradition would never die as long as an English villager had a hound or a fox laired up on the hill. Rufus loped wearily westward, alone. Rusty and his new-found mate curled up, cheek against cheek and slept in the heather as dawn silvered Hortonmere and the sun stippled the fells and touched the sleeping foxes with burnished glory.

BREED OF GIANTS
by JOYCE STRANGER

Few of those who have seen the Shire Personality of the Year, standing splendid in the spotlight at the Horse of the Year Show, dwarfing the herald's more delicate mounts, will ever forget the giant horse – proud and handsome, head held high, mane brilliant with tiny standards, tail braided with ribbons.

This book tells the story of John Johnson, a farmer, who breeds his gigantic Shire horses and, with fanatical devotion brings them up to championship status, only to have his hopes shattered by an accident to his best horse and an outbreak of foot-and-mouth disease on a neighbouring farm.

How Josh copes with his burdens and builds once more his winning strain of Shires, is told with all Joyce Stranger's skill and charm.

0 552 09893 0—85p

THE MONASTERY CAT AND OTHER ANIMALS
by JOYCE STRANGER

Here, from Joyce Stranger, Britain's best-loved writer of animal stories, are all the animals that she understands and describes so well ... pedigree cats and barnyard strays, working dogs and family pets, wild horses and untamed animals from the sea and the jungle ...

Joyce Stranger can write about animals as no other writer – and makes you love them ...

0 552 12044 8—£1.50

JOYCE STRANGER NOVELS AVAILABLE
IN CORGI PAPERBACKS

WHILE EVERY EFFORT IS MADE TO KEEP PRICES LOW, IT IS SOME-
TIMES NECESSARY TO INCREASE PRICES AT SHORT NOTICE. CORGI
BOOKS RESERVE THE RIGHT TO SHOW NEW RETAIL PRICES ON
COVERS WHICH MAY DIFFER FROM THOSE PREVIOUSLY ADVERTISED
IN THE TEXT OR ELSEWHERE.

THE PRICES SHOWN BELOW WERE CORRECT AT THE TIME OF GOING
TO PRESS (FEBRUARY '83).

☐ 12044 8	**THE MONASTERY CAT AND OTHER ANIMALS**	£1.50
☐ 11951 2	**THREE'S A PACK**	£1.50
☐ 09893 0	**BREED OF GIANTS**	85p
☐ 11803 6	**HOW TO OWN A SENSIBLE DOG (NF)**	£1.25
☐ 08141 8	**REX**	£1.25
☐ 08394 1	**CASEY**	£1.25
☐ 08633 9	**RUSTY**	£1.25
☐ 08931 1	**ZARA**	£1.25
☐ 10685 2	**FLASH**	£1.25
☐ 10695 X	**KYM**	£1.25

*All these books are available at your book shop or newsagent, or can be ordered
direct from the publisher. Just tick the titles you want and fill in the form below.*

CORGI BOOKS, Cash Sales Department, P.O. Box 11, Falmouth, Cornwall.

Please send cheque or postal order, no currency.

Please allow cost of book(s) plus the following for postage and packing:

U.K. Customers—Allow 45p for the first book, 20p for the second book and 14p for
each additional book ordered, to a maximum charge of £1.63.

B.F.P.O. and Eire—Allow 45p for the first book, 20p for the second book plus 14p per
copy for the next 7 books, thereafter 8p per book.

Overseas Customers—Allow 75p for the first book and 21p per copy for each
additional book.

NAME (Block Letters) ....

ADDRESS ....

....